D1351647

TO LOVE IS TO BE
HAPPY WITH

HUMAN HORIZONS SERIES

TO LOVE IS TO BE HAPPY WITH

Barry Neil Kaufman

A CONDOR BOOK
SOUVENIR PRESS (E&A) LTD

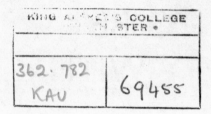

To
SUZI
the fountain, the love and the fire
. . . it begins with you

To
RAUN KAHLIL
you touched us and moved us
. . . in loving you, we found the way

To
BRYN and THEA
my very special little girls
. . . an inspiration each and every day

—To Nancy, Maire, Vikki, Laura and Jerry; you cared by giving us the best of yourselves and made it happen for Raun and for us.—To Abraham; thank you for giving me my part of the rock.—To Marv; my loving mentor who was always there without conditions or judgments.—To Elise, who gave me the stars.—To Bruce, who opened all the doors.—To the Attitude; "to love is to be happy with," without which we could not have begun.

—And to every child everywhere who wants a chance.

One

His little hands hold the plate delicately, his eyes surveying its smooth perimeter, and his mouth curls in delight. He is setting the stage . . . this is his moment as was the last and each before. This is the beginning of his entry into the solitude that has become his world. Slowly, with a masterful hand, he places the edge of the plate to the floor, sets his body in a comfortable and balanced position and snaps his wrist with great expertise. The plate begins to spin with dazzling perfection. It revolves on itself as if set into motion by some exacting machine. And it was.

This is not an isolated act, not a mere aspect of some childhood fantasy . . . it is a great and skilled activity performed by a very little boy for a very great and expectant audience—himself.

As the plate moves swiftly, spinning hypnotically on its edge, the little boy bends over it and stares squarely into its motion. Homage to himself, to the plate. For a moment, the boy's body betrays a just-perceptible motion similar to the plate's. For a moment, the little boy and his spinning creation become one. His eyes sparkle. He swoons in the playland that is himself. Alive. Alive.

1

Raun Kahlil . . . a little man occupying the edge of the universe.

Before this time, this very moment, we had always been in awe of Raun, our notably special child. We sometimes referred to him as "brain-blessed." He had always seemed to be riding the high of his own happiness. Highly-evolved. Seldom did he cry or utter tones of discomfort. In almost every way, his contentment and solitude seemed to suggest a profound and inner peace. He was a seventeen-month-old Buddha contemplating another dimension.

A little boy set adrift on the circulation of his own system. Encapsulated behind an invisible and seemingly inpenetrable wall. Soon he would be labeled. A tragedy. Unreachable. Bizarre. Statistically, he would fall into a category reserved for all those we see as hopeless . . . unapproachable . . . irreversible. For us the question: could we kiss the ground that the others had cursed?

*   *   *

The beginning. Only a year and five months ago. It was five-fifteen in the afternoon, a time when leaving New York City for home is like trying to pass through mechanized quicksand. Outside, the rush of metal monsters and the scattered hustle of fast-walking, blank-faced people pushing toward their daily release. The rush-hour climax. The last ejaculation of energy to be spent in the day.

And me sitting quietly in my office on Sixth Avenue, playing the tick-tack-toe of advertising with another film—now Fellini, sometimes Bergman, a Dustin Hoffman film, even James Bond. Developing the concept, the image and the essence of a consumer ad campaign. Reams of sketch-pad paper in front of me covered with doodles of a thousand ideas. Doing it again and again. Absorbed in the challenge of positioning a product in the marketplace, I was feeling high on the freedom to originate and create. Turning the words. Hypothesizing the pictures and graphics. Mothering their execution in photography, sculpture or illustration. This was the birthplace of my favored ideas which survived and the graveyard for the ads that fell before

2

commercial firing squads and bled to death on the floors of smoke-filled conference rooms.

Now I was contemplating the solution to another project while preparing for my daily hustle through the crowd of humanity. Home to Suzi, whose warm embrace would be a soothing nightcap to my day. To Bryn, my seven-year-old sexy lady who does Chaplinesque routines at the drop of a hat. To Thea, whose dark eyes and tiny three-year-old form announces the presence of a little mystic. To crazy Sasha and majestic Riguette, big, bold, bearlike 130-pound Belgian herding dogs that have a striking resemblance to me.

Suddenly, the piercing ring of the telephone crashes through my veil of concentration. The buzzer rings . . . for me.

"Now . . . it just started, and already the contractions are only four minutes apart. I'll get someone to watch the girls and somebody else to take me to the hospital. Are you okay? Don't get upset. Just take your time. I'll wait for you. Everything will be okay . . . the nurses are trained and they'll help me until you get there."

Suzi seemed so in control. The waves of excitement heaved through my body. Not now, Jesus, not now during the rush hour. As I flew down the stairs, I chuckled at the irony. Months of practice. Together. Unlike the birth of our other children, this would be a joint project, a birth for both Suzi and me. Natural. We were following the Lamaze method, no drugs, no painkillers. Father and mother would be joined in numbers and patterns of breathing. We were both graduates of an elaborate training program so that each of us could function together from the beginning of labor through the actual delivery. In this beautiful process, I was to be an essential part. But first I had to get there . . . to be with her.

Panic. I would never make it through the maze. To support her; to love her; to consummate the creation. The stop-start of the car. The memories flashed by in a slow-motion montage. Move it. Move it faster. My pulse pounded in my head as if to help the forward momentum. Push it. Will it. Wish the traffic away. I imagined Suzi all alone in some cold and drafty tiled room . . . counting and breathing to her own echoes. All the practice, the patience . . . robbed by some cruel and arbitrary set of circumstances. Impossible. I would not let it be.

My mind outpaced the car. For Suzi, this was not just the birth of our third. It was the culmination of a dream. To share this experience with me. To have me as part of this evolution. And to have a son. She had conspired with her doctor and they had both agreed that it would be a boy. Our first boy. The girls had filled our lives with new loving and softness. For me, another lady in the house would be sensational. A boy would be an unexpected gift. For Suzi, the emotional investment was different. She loved the girls with an abiding intensity, but she had always wanted at least one male child. And now she felt sure she could add that specialness to her life.

My hands began to stick to the wheel . . . one hour had elapsed. Snapped from me, from us. I pulled the car onto the grass and pushed at the accelerator. Up, over the curbs. The endless patterns of stilled automobiles at my side. Jumping the lights. A daylight phantom moving the molecules. Pushing it.

I had to be there. I knew that I was more than just a significant member of the cast, I was the only one left to her. Suzi's father was distant and unavailable, consumed by a second marriage and a new family of young children. Four years ago her mother had died at the early age of forty-six while developing the fruits of her second marriage. Her sister remains on the other side of a wall. Like Suzi, she too had to endure the lonely years of a childhood immersed in confusion and divorce. The pain and the anguish had splashed up against both of them. But Suzi had also reached for the loving and the joy. All these years repairing the damage, reconstructing herself and finding new alternatives. It had been a difficult and inconsistent journey for her in her time. And for me, in mine. But most of it was just a memory now, clouded in the frosted lens of another era. With each other, we had found new reasons to be.

Finally . . . the hospital. I parked haphazardly and literally bolted from the car. Sprinting up the lawn, jumping three steps at a time, through the entrance and a mad dash for an opened elevator. Down the long hallways. People scattering out of my way . . . not so much because they sensed my urgency, but for their own survival. This was a tight-quartered version of a football scrimmage. My six-foot-three frame carrying its two hundred and twenty-five pounds as I charged forcefully through

4

the interior of this public building. Catching the imagery of a metaphysical quarterback reincarnated as a Grizzly Bear, with thick, wild hair flying behind and a bearded face bounding up and down to the rhythm of the loping movement. The Big Bear. A nickname Suzi and my daughters had blessed me with, their lyrical and affectionate interpretation of my appearance and size. Barry . . . became Barz, which became Bears, which finally became "The Big Bear." Me. In my mad, comic-book surge, still dodging and running over the polished floor, gliding high on my own energy.

Then it came to me . . . a voice, my name bouncing off the floor and walls. From the distance, a nurse frantically waved me on as if she were cheering a long shot in the last race at Aqueduct. And for me, it was the last couple of yards, the finish line for the long-distance runner.

No time now. Undress in the hallway. Our child was about to be born. I had just made it.

"Is she okay?"

"She's doing just fine."

Now another nurse was helping . . . holding out the white garb and face mask, taking off my shoes.

Suzi had in some way decided to wait for me and not to abandon natural childbirth by taking the needle . . . and drifting away. But, if need be, she would have done it alone. She had trusted herself.

There were screams from the other rooms; the symphony of labor out of control. I floated: Into a quiet cubicle, finally at Suzi's side . . . another nurse giving me my wife's hand. She was in the middle of a contraction. Her stomach arched upward into a tall mound while her lips were puckered. She rapidly pushed air in and out of her lungs in short, shallow beats. Intense. Quiet. A beautiful pantomime.

At first she didn't look at me, but I knew that she knew I was there. She pressed her hand tightly into mine as I kissed her lightly; then both of us started counting out loud. The corners of her mouth wrinkled in a slightly formed smile.

Down the corridor into the delivery room. White-tiled walls, aluminum instruments and bright lights. More panting. We talked between the eruptions. More frantic than we had imagined, but we were both with it. Even the doctor was riding the

5

high of the moment, humming some vaguely-familiar romantic Italian tune he might have heard in his childhood. The nurses moved quickly into different positions. Everyone was preparing for their role. The performance in a very contemporary play . . . a theatrical event.

Episiotomy. No one in the class for natural childbirth had ever mentioned that—the cutting. As I watched, the room began to dance before my eyes. Then it began swirling. The image of myself became fractured and began to crumble. Someone grabbed me as I fell forward and led me from the room. The nurse smiled and told me that it happens all the time. But it didn't matter. I could not miss it now. I tucked some smelling salts under my face mask and sneaked back in. Everyone smiled. Suzi seemed so intense, so very much in control. She giggled as I returned to her side and then was quickly lost in the next contraction.

The doctor told her to push now . . . with everything she had. My insides were pushing with her. She seemed so courageous to me now. No cries of pain. No misgivings. She was totally involved. A creator and participant. Suddenly, after a gigantic thrust, a beautiful steel-gray child slipped from the womb of her body. A boy. He began to breathe and cry at the same time. The doctor put him on Suzi's stomach as he severed the umbilical cord. Unbelievable. He was ours and we had seen him come into life.

The nurse called him a perfect specimen. We looked at each other in awe. Each second, the color in his face and body changed. As he took in air, the misty gray became pink and his wide-eyed glance beheld the universe. Tears fell from Suzi's eyes. Joyful. The culmination. I felt so alive . . . so connected. We would call him Raun Kahlil.

*   *   *

At home, the first month with Raun was not quite what we had expected or wanted. He seemed troubled, crying day and night. He was unresponsive to being held or fed, as if preoccupied with some internal turmoil. We shuttled back and forth to the doctor, receiving assurances that our baby was perfectly healthy and normal. The Apgar rating was 10 at birth, the

6

highest possible score an infant can obtain for alertness and reflexes. Yet Suzi still sensed that something was definitely wrong. Her intuitive grasp kept us both alert.

Then, in the fourth week of his life, a severe ear infection suddenly surfaced. Again, we turned to the doctor, who prescribed antibiotics. But the crying continued. And continued. The doctor increased the medication.

The infection began to spread like lava moving through both ears and into his throat. An apparent minor condition of dehydration resulting from the antibiotics escalated into a critical condition. Raun began to lose the spark of life. His eyelids were at half-mast. His movements became lethargic. Suzi pursued the pediatrician, describing Raun's symptoms and situation. The doctor wanted to wait another day, explaining that our son's current condition could be a normal response to the medicine. Yet Suzi wanted Raun checked immediately, and upon her insistence, the doctor agreed. Since house calls were no longer fashionable, she had to wrap our sick baby in blankets and transport him to the doctor's office. She raced through the streets, manipulating and darting through traffic as she realized that, though Raun was breathing normally, his skin had begun to take on a white pallor.

The doctor was aghast and amazed. He had not anticipated that the dehydration would become so severe. Raun slipped behind his closed eyelids; even the doctor could not rouse a movement from him. Preparation was made for immediate emergency hospitalization. Our son was placed in a pediatric intensive-care unit. His name appeared on the critical list. Everything happened so rapidly, it was like moving through a blur of uncontrollable events.

Our visits were short and confined as dictated by hospital rules. Raun was locked in a plastic isolette, hidden from us, lost in a mechanized world of tubes and glass. Suzi and I had to dress in sterile white gowns. We bathed our hands and faces in an iodine solution as a sterilizing precaution. Although permitted in his glass cubicle, we were not allowed to touch our son. We watched, feeling helpless, as if we had been thrust out of the picture. We knew we could lose him.

All around us there were little infants connected to wires and pumps which maintained their tenuous lifelines. In the next booth, a young nurse wearing rubber gloves pushed her hands through the special holes in the side of an isolette. The little girl inside moved restlessly as the young woman worked with great precision and premeditation, adjusting all the valves and devices. Suddenly, the nurse stopped her activity as if awakened from a dream. She looked directly at the baby and smiled at her. Then, placing her face within inches of the plastic container, she began to sing as she softly caressed the infant's belly with her rubberized hands. The little girl's movements became less erratic. Her tiny fingers clutched the nurse's hand. The two of them touched each other in a beautiful vignette of caring—of remembering to care.

This scene lifted our spirits for Raun and all the other children confined to the unit. Each day when we returned, we were given guarded forecasts. Although his ear infection was serious, it was the heavy medication that had created the current crisis. My mind flexed. The same people who had caused the dehydration were now feverishly trying to reverse its effect. How could we know what to do? What judgments could we make? We were lost in a crowd of charts, injections and questions.

Several days passed with us all at the edge of a cliff; hanging on. Early-morning coffee as Suzi and I sat silently with each other, avoiding the view of the empty crib. But we were bursting with emotions and the intensity of those feelings broke the quiet, which always seemed so powerful. We held on to Raun through conversations about him and by sharing our acute sensitivity and love toward him.

Afternoons and evenings were spent at the hospital. On the fifth day, we heard the first really optimistic forecast. He would get through it. At last, he was holding food and his weight was stabilized. But, unfortunately, the infection had caused damage. Both his eardrums had ruptured from the pressure of the fluids, which could result in a possible loss or impairment of hearing. For us, it would not matter. If Raun was deaf or partially deaf, we would find a way to pump the world's music into his head. All that mattered was that he was alive and thriving again.

Happily, we embarked on our second beginning at home. Raun was a new child with no more pain. He smiled all the time.

Free from the difficulties that characterized his first month, he was blissful, alert and responsive. He was eating well and loving the world. We felt alive again, together again. The nightmare had given birth to a new morning.

As we settled in, Suzi and I turned our focus to the girls . . . wanting to be sensitive to their wants and needs, their contending with this new presence in our home. Bryn was beautiful, intense, and dramatic. An extrovert who was so verbal and articulate she often crossed the line from the profound into the obnoxious. More a friend and companion than a daughter. For her, Raun was not simply her brother; this child was her child. He would replace the dolls and the afternoon fantasies.

For Thea, the circumstances were very different. Artistic and moody, unpredictable and mysterious, she now had the distinction of becoming the middle child. This was the onerous position I had held with uneasiness in my family. She was not the first to be cuddled and break new ground. She was no longer the youngest child, to be the endless and eternal baby, who usually reaps a fantastic harvest of attention. Thea had been dethroned by Raun. We were concerned that she might feel displaced and dislodged. For her, we wanted to provide special and extra doses of overt attention and love. We would give her more now so that she could continue to develop in her very particular and individual style.

The first year of Raun's life whizzed by with incredible speed. He grew more and more beautiful. Smiling, laughing and playing as the girls had. Even his hearing seemed appropriate, his listening to voices and turning his head toward various sounds. With the exception of not putting his arms out to be picked up, Raun seemed normal and healthy in every way.

When he was a year old, we began to note increasing audio insensitivity. He showed less and less response to his name and to general sounds. It was as though his hearing were progressively diminishing. Each week, he seemed to become more and more aloof. We knew there was the possibility that he might have a hearing deficiency. Perhaps there was something we could do to help him, something we could provide. We had his hearing checked. Although it was too early to determine hearing loss accurately, the doctor asserted that despite the possibility of deafness, Raun was in "good shape," that his inconsistent

9

aloofness was of no great concern. He insisted that our son would outgrow any peculiarities.

Over the next four months, Raun's supposed or possible hearing deficit became compounded by his tendency to stare and to be passive. He seemed to prefer solitary play rather than interaction with our family. When we picked him up, his arms casually dangled at his sides as if they were disconnected from his body. Often, he expressed dislike or discomfort with physical contact by pushing our hands away from his body when we tried to embrace or fondle him. He demonstrated a preference for sameness and routine, consistently choosing one or two objects to play with and going to a special area in the house to sit by himself.

And then some obvious inconsistencies appeared in regard to his hearing capability. He would not hear a loud and sharp noise close to him, but might be attentive to a soft and distant sound. Then, at other times, a noise that he had not reacted to previously would suddenly attract his attention.

Even the sounds he made and the one or two words that he had mimicked were no longer part of his repertoire. Instead of acquiring language, he had become mute. Even a prelinguistic language of pointing or gesturing did not exist.

We took him back to the hospital. After repeated examinations for audio receptivity, we were informed that Raun could hear, but that his seemingly strange, aloof and obtuse behavior made proper diagnosis difficult. At one point during a test, when the technicians bombarded Raun with a special sequence of tones, he did not react at all. In fact, because there were not even reflexive responses in his eyes or eyelids, it seemed as if he were deaf. About ten minutes later, however, while he was facing the wall between exercises, he began to repeat the notes he had heard before in the exact pitch and sequence in which they were played. To the amazement of everyone, our son, whose lack of reactions was akin to that of a deaf child, could indeed hear. But the consistency and the quality of his intake and what he was capable of doing with his audio reception were open to question.

Sunday afternoon as the sun bleaches the grass into warm yellows. A father and a son, together in the park. A twentieth-century Rembrandt canvas. I watched him as the swing carried

10

him back and forth. With new eyes, I viewed a child who I was now convinced could hear, perhaps even perfectly. I addressed him, as I often did, as a peer. Talking directly to him. "Why?" I asked. What was happening to him? To us? Somehow, I knew that he could make some sense out of my ramblings . . . a little big man with profoundly gigantic sensibilities. I kept speaking. I wanted him to help me know more about his specialness. Deaf ears . . . mute. Seemingly inattentive. And yet was his lack of response really the sign?

He kept looking at me, through me. His eyes did not seem to absorb my image, but merely reflected it back to me. Again I asked him, but it was like asking the wind. And every time I looked at my son I found myself turning inward. Searching within myself for the answer.

And finally my thoughts began to flow . . . the cataloging, the laying bare of the particulars that were Raun Kahlil. The rocking back and forth on the leverage of his own eternity. The soft and gentle retreat to the outside perimeter of our world. The spinning and the fixed stare. His great agility and his hypnotic fascination with inanimate objects. The self-stimulated smile and the repetitious motion of his fingers against his lips. The pushing-away of people and the silent aloneness. When Raun turned to you, he turned through you as if you were transparent.

And, then the keen awareness that he did not use language. Not just a slow talker, he offered no communication by sound or gesture, no expression of wants, likes or dislikes. Almost one and a half years old . . . Raun, a new creature in a strange land.

Standing in the playground, I meditated and allowed my ideas to drift freely in my mind. I sifted through them as my internal wandering brought me closer to a conclusion. I looked again at Raun; he was so far away. The wooden seat of the swing and its chains had become a substitute for the plate that he would often set into motion by spinning. It was merely another moving vehicle that facilitated his exquisite ride into a quietly personal and solitary universe.

I called to him and heard the echo in his valley. I laughed and caught the fantasy of an imagined smile. I spoke again. This time, he turned his eyes toward me, and for a fleeting and barely perceptible moment we made contact. Then he was

11

gone again. Blond hair in Shirley Temple ringlets, large brown riveted eyes reflecting my image back to me.

A word appeared like a neon sign on the surface of my thoughts. A label which was confusing, frightening and bizarre. I pushed at it, focusing my mind's eye on it. Then I drew away and tried to shake it loose. I gazed again at Raun. His softness recharged me. I brought the word into sharper focus. It danced in my head like a vulture inviting me to the last resort. Yet it would be my last resort, my private vision, my choice to make it madness. The word became undeniable and I mouthed it into existence.

Autism . . . infantile autism. A subcategory of childhood schizophrenia . . . the most irreversible category of the profoundly disturbed and psychotic. Could the word destroy the dream, forever limiting the horizons of my son, and damn him to a deviant and sealed corner of our lives?

Just a hypothesis, yet it seemed correct. As I continued to observe my son, all the vague and distant memory data of my education were rekindled. Scattered pieces of information surfaced. Elements of an indefinite puzzle. Maybe my memory units were imperfect and misleading. I swept Raun off the swing onto the back seat of the bicycle. As I pedaled toward home, I sensed that my supposition was correct.

Like a junkie looking for his angry fix, I searched the cavity of my mind, hoping for a doorway out. There was a difference; the pattern wasn't complete. Raun was always happy and peaceful, seemingly caught in the mellow hue of a thousand years of meditation. This serenity placed him outside the classic form of autism, which generally was characterized by unhappy and even angry children.

I submerged myself in this revelation for the remainder of the day. Evening and the last dance. Suzi, Bryn, and Thea played out their final chorus of the day, punctuated with ten "goodnights," "five-more-minute" pleas and much jumping up and down. The smiles and the pretended sighs. Four hundred kisses were given, each one calculated to buy more time, to delay the inevitable—the ultimate evening trip to their beds. The girls manipulated and meandered while Suzi coaxed and herded them to the stairs as she completed the last chores of the day. It was a choreographed ballet performed each evening to my delight. Three women, alive and animated. Raun, off to the side by his own movement, was quiet, peaceful and disconnected.

As I waited for Suzi to finish, I rehearsed the word. I said it softly and quietly to myself. I uttered it with authority and conviction. I phrased it as a question. Yes, that would be the way . . . just a question.

When she returned, she sat opposite me and faced me with a foreboding directness. It was as if she knew that I wanted to talk and that my words would be heavy. The energy flowed from my mouth and rambled over unfamiliar territory. Finally, the word "autism" crept from between my lips. Suzi didn't flinch. She listened carefully to my hypothesis. Her clear blue eyes sparkled with an eagerness to know . . . to understand . . . to pin it down so that at least we could move on. Her long blond hair curled softly over her shoulders, while her fingers moved slowly across her bottom lip as her forehead furrowed. The light dipped in and out of the shallow crevices of her face. We looked at each other through the mist in our eyes.

Sitting there together in the living room, we were silent as the word "autism" settled into the space and spread out around us. It had so much power that I knew Suzi needed a couple of minutes by herself to absorb it. As I waited, my eyes traveled from one object to another . . . stopping at our woodcut of a four-hundred-year-old man . . . then to "Anguish," a piece of sculpture gouged out of onyx. Our house had always been a collection of ourselves. The toilet bowl I painted in honor of Suzi's last birthday. Her charcoal portrait of my face, which she had given to me three years ago from a hospital bed after suffering injuries in a horseback-riding accident.

I smiled at the great Murray, which I created one weekend out of surgical bandage wrapped around an armature—a life-size, chalk-white figure who sits peacefully in a reconditioned barber chair from the early part of this century and holds in his hands an opened copy of Walt Whitman's *Leaves of Grass.* Seven bronze figures of Yosemite sit on a glass table. A gift given to us eight years ago by our friend who sits in California battling with his downbeat and painful version of the artistic life. The nine-foot construction I designed and formed out of antique wood type. And Suzi's imposing acrylics . . . forms and images

13

chiseled out of clear lucite. Dense and transparent at the same time. Intense and mystifying statements. Some original photography which were rejects from my creative endeavors in advertising, decorated the walls.

Lifting my feet onto the coffee table, I recalled that even it had a story . . . once a hatch door on a World War II Liberty ship which carried troops across the Atlantic. I was immersed in the richness of our lives. The objects were wonderful footnotes for where we had been, what we had done and how we had felt. They represented an evolution of eleven years, that at times had been unpredictable and vulnerable. Those difficult first years, with their up-and-down inconsistencies. The last several years of coming together. Now, just as it seemed to be almost perfect, we found ourselves contemplating the impossible; the something that always happens to someone else, never you. We confronted a reality which could last for a lifetime and turn it all into a tragedy.

Suzi's teal-blue eyes had been fixed on some indeterminate point in space. Her radiant face was framed by the gentle flow of her hair. Her trim figure was clothed in old blue jeans, its denim decorated with leather and Indian-print patches, and a long-sleeved polo shirt embroidered with roses and an art deco landscape. She was in full bloom, deep and sensuous. Yet the infectious way she would laugh while sitting cross-legged in the middle of the floor or the way she would jump into the air to dance to some outrageous tune on the radio suggested a more adolescent and childlike inclination . . . a soft pink scent of jasmine and the sunshine of a teenager exploring her femininity. Even now in this shadow, her lust for living danced on the surface. She turned toward me and exhaled a long sigh, letting her head rock up and down as if to say over and over again: "Yes, I know. I know."

Together, we decided to explore and research the subject. It had always been her belief that Raun could hear and that "something else" was happening with him. We pulled out the old psychology books with their scribbled messages from another era. We took new books from the library. Finally, we had it. Leo Kanner had labeled it first in 1943. Others expanded the initial criteria and a constellation of symptoms were recorded. Autism is an illness not defined by origin or cause, but by a

14

collection of associated symptoms or behavior.

The categories: antisocial and aloof patterns of activity, hypnotic preoccupation with spinning, rocking and repetitive movements, no verbal communication and sometimes no prelinguistic gesture language, the appearance of looking through people, fascination with inanimate objects, no anticipatory gestures when being approached or picked up, often seems deaf, unresponsive and self-stimulating, desirous of sameness and pushes off from physical contact. Generally, for no apparent reason, they are physically attractive children. Thirty years ago, this man had described our infant son. Raun fit every category with the exception of being self-destructive (banging his head and so on).

Suzi and I looked at each other. For a while we searched for each other's reaction. We explored our fears, our feeling of despair and the seeming enormity of our discovery. We would try to make it all right. We would see it through. If Raun was autistic, we would help him. We would love him. We would, with his sisters, find a way.

The literature argued against our optimistic mood. The literature talked about the noncommunicative child who most often slips behind a veil of his own solitude and becomes unreachable. Bruno Bettelheim, in *The Empty Fortress*, describes autism as trauma and articulates the pessimistic results of his study. The overwhelming percentage of these children were hospitalized and confined to custodial care for their entire lives. Their personalities disintegrated (or never developed) and the family units or environments crumbled. Bettelheim noted the few he had reached, but ultimately almost all showed severely limited communicative and adaptive abilities. His vision of causality included an indictment of the parents, for he believed that these children were protesting a cold and unresponsive environment. So much of what he said was judgmental; his defining of all autistic behavior as symptoms and statements the child supposedly made in regard to his immediate environment.

We also noted all the inconsistencies and the poor success rate with these children . . . a success measured by some abstract curve of normalcy. We had to stay open—there was too much to absorb and too much to learn to start drawing conclusions. We wanted to stay free of fearing the future so we could understand what was happening to us and our child.

Suzi began the endless telephone conversations with professionals. Their advice was usually abrupt and contradictory. "He's too young." "We never see them so young." "Go here; go there." "Hopeless." "Great, what we really want is to get them young." "Give him a full psychiatric evaluation." "Face it now! He'll probably have to be institutionalized." "He'll need a neurological work-up and an EEG." "He'll probably outgrow it." "It could be a tumor . . . a brain tumor." "We know so little about autism." "There's not much we can do; bring him to us in a year." "Unfortunately, we know very little about these kinds of children."

We had talks with doctors and hospitals in and around New York City. We queried an institute in Philadelphia specializing in brain-damaged and autistic children. There were the specialized environmental schools, one in Brooklyn and one in Nassau County, neither of which would see our child until he was much older—and even then it would be a "maybe." We contacted a dedicated specialist in behaviorism in California with a major university and a Federal grant to study and research autism. We investigated psycho-pharmacology. Psychoanalysis. Behaviorism. Vitamin therapy. Nutritional analysis. The CNS (central nervous system) factor. The genetic theory. There were many opinions and non-opinions, many unsubstantiated theories and debatable assumptions.

As Suzi's informational grip spread out over the country, I withdrew into my hermitage of solitude to read everything available on the subject. I examined, in depth, the writings of Carl Delacato and his concepts of patterning and sensory impairment. He believed that autistic children are not psychotic as Bettelheim described them, but defined them as brain-damaged, with perceptual dysfunctions.

Reading incessantly, I probed the psychoanalytic themes. Scrutinized I. Newton Kugelmass. Explored the writings and research of the articulate and incisive Bernard Rimland, his concept of impaired cognitive function; the inability of these children to relate new stimuli to old, remembered data. Studied Martin Kozloff and his thesis of operant conditioning. I delved into behavior modification, where they ignore causality and meaning in favor of restructuring these children's lives by de-

16

signing a thorough and complex system of rewards and punishments. Was this an exercise in robotizing these children?

Considered Dr. Ivar Lovaas and his search for hope among the hopeless. I had developed an intense respect for his dedication and research, but had difficulty accepting some of his basic premises. Jumped back into B. F. Skinner and even Freud. The mountain of writing was extensive and contradictory. Observation, statistics, theories and speculation. In antiquity, Raun would have been considered as blessed by the "divine disease."

We tried to pull it together, to make some sense out of the miasma of volumes and lengthy telephone conversations. We were trying to synthesize a direction.

We decided to have an examination and work-up done on Raun. He was almost seventeen months old. We had to plunge in somewhere, but at least now we felt more knowledgeable. First, we arranged for an interview and an analysis at a major institution with a highly renowned psychiatric division. They confirmed our son's serious developmental problems and bizarre autistic behavior patterns, but they did not want to label him. They believed that often labels were self-fulfilling prophesies. We were told that if autism was officially diagnosed, our son's records could precipitate his being excluded from certain school systems and programs and that many other professionals often treat such children as hopelessly limited in potential. Come back in a year and they would have another look at him. We were disappointed . . . even angry. We wanted help, not an abstract diagnosis.

Another hospital, two more work-ups and then the word "autism" was again used. There were expressions of surprise at our ability to detect the autistic symptoms in a child so young since usually such signs are not fully recognized before children are two and a half to three years old. And yet, for us, the bizarre and unusual behavior was so pronounced that there was no way we could not acknowledge that something was terribly wrong.

The doctors were again solicitous and kind. They were empathetic and appeared concerned. As after the first examination, we were told to return in nine months to a year. Why nine months? Not because Raun couldn't be worked with, but because their affiliated facilities do not deal with children so young. A child with these symptoms normally is three or four

17

years old before he is given any professional help. We pushed. Could they make an exception? We wanted help now. Under the pressure of our persistence, one of the doctors suggested we call them after the summer. She promised to try to help us then, but this was the best they could do for us now.

Again, we received no concrete help, but our diagnosis was once more confirmed.

The letdown. After all this insanity of effort, we were told exactly what we already knew. By now we were not looking for more confirmations. To verbally suggest that the earlier you get this type of child, the better, and then to actually turn the child away because he is too young seemed cruel and self-defeating. Depressing statistics or depressing attitudes? Why should the doctors rush if they believe that autism is irreversible and incurable?

We felt we had to intervene and do it now. Each day we could see him slipping from us, withdrawing. Becoming more insensitive to audio and visual stimuli. Becoming more encapsulated. Raun seemed bewildered too. Medical and institutional help was not available. The benign and futile gesture of endless finger pointing by the professionals was incredibly trying and unconstructive. After contacting the National Society for Autistic Children and talking with parents of children similar to ours, we found that most had initiated a search for information and advice and received little or no help. In many instances, they learned to accept their predicaments with varying degrees of despair and frustration.

But we believed in Raun . . . in his peace, in his beauty and in his happiness.

We knew that now it was up to us and to him. Perhaps it had always been that way. All the diagnostic confirmations and analyses might have statistical meaning to a number-hungry society, but not to a little boy with staring eyes. If Raun was to get help, if this little autistic boy could be reached and brought into our world, it would have to be done now and by us alone. Now, while he was young. Now, while we were wanting. Now, while he was still happy in his infantile playland.

If we waited, we were convinced that he would become just another dismal statistic. We knew that the game would have to be played out while Raun's behavior patterns were still new and unentrenched, while his difficulty with approaching his environment had not as yet created serious emotional problems, while his peace and his joy were pristine and unspoiled.

We had little to work with but our own deep desire to reach Raun, to help him reach out to us. The professionals offered no real hope or help, but in our love for our son and his beauty we had found a determination to persist.

Two

Where to begin? We decided to start with ourselves . . . with the evolution of our own beliefs and feelings.

It was like taking a pilgrimage back in order to come forward. Searching and sifting through the nostalgia of my recent past in hopes of recrystallizing the knowledge. I thought back to the mid-1960s, when I graduated from college with a degree in philosophy. I remembered the months and years of flexing the membranes of my mind. The infinity of questions and the near answers. Then, graduate work in psychology. I was lost in a world in which I listened, accepting the confusion, never believing that I could fully trust myself and move from my own awareness.

Built a barricade around my feelings as I helped nurse my dying mother in her last years. The rides to Manhattan for an endless series of cobalt-radiation treatments. I watched in agony as her world crumbled. I did not know then to talk with her about it and to tell her I knew it was almost over. We cluttered life with bedside smiles, chatter of trivia and fabricated busyness. I never told her how much I cared. We created a conspiracy of silence; a gesture we had envisioned as distinctly humane. But, in ʋur kindness, perhaps we had left her alone with her thoughts and fears. When the end came, my system erupted in an upheaval and a protest against the universe for taking her into its womb beyond my imagination. I screamed at myself through my sorrow for not being with her openly and loving her as the odor of death enveloped her.

Twenty-one ... and the walls came tumbling down. My eyes clouded over with a melancholy vision of existence. Seven years trudging to a lonely Park Avenue office to choke out slightly-abortive sessions with a Freudian psychoanalyst. Those were years of anguish and silence of free association and confusion. Searching for old elephant bones beneath the pillows of my unconscious. Pushing myself for alternatives and a new freedom. Trying to lift the weight off my shoulders. Finally finding some comfort and clarity, but it was still limited and tentative. Ideas and understanding seemed to fluctuate day by day. After seven years, I still felt trapped and dangling from the end of my rope.

Eventually, I terminated this analytical version of therapy with its half-measure vision of life. I can still remember the echo of a well-meaning psychiatrist who would tell his patients: "You will always have times when you are anxious and fearful ... but you are now better equipped to handle it, to cope." Disillusionment. This sounded like an intellectual and emotional compromise. To leave it, still with discomfort ... knowing there had to be more, if I could only find it.

My early dream had been to be a writer. To go beyond my walls with words and change perhaps just one person. To make that mark. An adolescent fantasy which I had thus far laid aside for a career in films and advertising. The second dream was different. A promise to myself that had become a real and viable secondary pursuit in the area of psychotherapy and education. I had considered a career in psychiatry once, but as I took a closer look, the medical model seemed inappropriate and obsolete. Graduate schools were cluttered and overburdened with brittle books and strange approximations of reality. The whisper within me said to focus on a perspective, search for a path and find the movement.

For some of these diverse explorations, which occurred during the first years of our marriage, Suzi would come too. A joint venture into what seemed to be an endless abyss. Into experiments with hypnosis and the continued exorcism of that second dream. Then, auto-hypnosis. For me, the tool became so exquisitely developed that I could put myself "under" by merely touching my forehead with my index finger. Beautiful, but incomplete. It was no panacea, but definitely a soothing internal massage.

Still before Raun. My appetite for answers was enormous. I read ferociously, consuming countless books, and experimented with new theories. Ideas and dogma. Freud. Jung. Adler. To Sullivan and Horney. On to Perls and the dramatic confrontations of Gestalt. Moving forward with Sartre and Kierkegaard. Deep into the simplicity and loving of Carl Rogers. Tipping the trinity of Eric Berne, beguiled by the theatrical and highly fascinating screams of Janov. Courses in group dynamics and the experience of interpersonal workshops. Fell in and out of Skinner rather quickly, but lingered with Maslow. Bathed in the quiet wisdom of Zen and then Yoga . . . searching for some new or old grip on reality.

Taoism. The beautifully perceptive teaching that "life is not going anywhere, because it is already here." Meditation. Confucius. "To know what you know and what you don't know is a characteristic of one who knows." On to the philosophical basis of acupuncture. Back into the collective unconsciousness of mankind and its genetic implications. All these were moving and arresting attempts to make sense out of the human condition. Philosophy, psychology, religion and mysticism. Enlightening, yet I knew to go on, knowing that there would be something someday that would rivet itself into the core and unravel the perplexities for me. Although I had acquired much, I chose to continue this purely personal pilgrimage.

Although I was growing more cynical, I still pushed forward. Until the day I sat in the classroom of a school that has since disappeared, and heard a man talking about something called the Option Method. He was a short, round, monk-like Friar Tuck sipping Coke and smoking one cigarette after another . . . concrete, incisive and illuminating.

As I listened, I felt a surging from within. Understanding a knowledge that always seemed to have been there, but that I had never really put into focus. As it crystallized rapidly for me, I began to recognize that my feelings and wants did come from my beliefs and that those beliefs could be investigated. And this pursuit of exposing and choosing beliefs was the subject of the Option Method, which was born out of the Option Attitude: "To love is to be happy with." It was not merely a philosophy, but a vision that would become the basis for our way of life and a foundation from which we would try to help Raun. This developing awareness enabled us to see our son and ourselves with great clarity and freedom.

Choice was really possible and the act of choosing was crucial. For the first time, old beliefs (like "I do not choose my feelings, they just come upon me" and "I am a victim of what happened to me in my past" and "I can't help it, that's just the way I am") were open to question.

I realized that the personality could be viewed as a constellation of beliefs. Between each event (whether it be real or imaginary, perceived or performed, etc.) and the reaction to it (whether it be fight or flight, fear or joy or neutrality), there is a belief. It is the underbelly of all our feelings and wants. Change the belief and you change the behavior as well as the feelings. So precisely simple and accurate that the ideas were disarming.

For the Option teacher or facilitator, there are no judgments to be made . . . no good or bad. No diagnosis. No directing toward specific goals but allowing each question to flow naturally from the student's previous statement or answer. Guiding others to help themselves see through unhappiness to the underlying beliefs. Dealing with the feelings we have which we do not seem to want, such as anxiety, fear, anger, frustration, insecurity, etc. To work with people by allowing them their self-direction, their verbal symbols and their private visions is an essential fundamental of the Method.

This kind of probe into the human dynamic revealed one profound commonalty in many of us: we believe that we have to be unhappy sometimes and that it is even good or productive to be unhappy. Our culture supports it. Unhappiness is the mark of sensitivity, the tattoo of a thinking man. It is considered by some to be the only "reasonable" and "human" response to a difficult and problematic world.

We can see this type of mechanism operating all the time; being unhappy or using it as a way to deal with ourselves, other

23

people and activities. We fear dying so that we can stop smoking. We dread rejection in order to motivate ourselves to stop eating and not become fatter. We become anxious as a way of pushing ourselves to work harder and achieve more. We get headaches in order to have a reason to avoid something we don't want to do. We feel guilty to punish ourselves in order to prevent ourselves from doing the same things in the future. We get unhappy when someone we love is unhappy in order to show them how much we care. We get angry at our co-workers to make them move faster.

We punish in order to prevent. We hate war in order to stay in touch with our desire for peace. We fear death in order to live.

These are just some of the pressures we might put on ourselves in order to stay in touch with what we want or to motivate ourselves to get more . . . all this so that eventually we can be happy or fulfilled. Ultimately these dynamics become part of the sophisticated internal systems by which we function.

I remember a fascinating incident with Thea when she was about three years old. She came to us quietly one afternoon and asked for candy. Since we did not keep candy in the house and it would have required going to a store when we were busy, her request was denied. Perhaps, we suggested, we could buy her the candy another time. But, for this determined and resourceful young lady, our response was not satisfactory. Consistent with the fiber of her personality, she persisted. Her initial, gentle request turned into a series of pleas. Whining was accompanied by grimaces. Her posture stiffened and her body movements became perceptibly frenetic. Thea might have been preparing for some great challenge or battle.

Still concerned with not achieving her goal, Thea escalated her efforts by demanding the candy. She substantiated those demands with a complex succession of arguments. Again we explained our situation. Suzi stroked Thea's hair and told the little dynamo how much we loved her. For just a moment Thea relaxed and seemed satisfied. But then she decided to pay the highest tribute to her wanting and started to cry. It was astounding to watch the progression of her efforts. She was working very hard.

I did not want her to be unhappy, so I sat beside her, letting my fingers dance all over her belly and tickling her under her arms. As she began to smile and allow herself to giggle, she pushed my hands away. Then, as I continued, she moved to the other side of the room in protest. For two frozen seconds, she looked at me through her tears and another smile broke through the clouds of her "unhappiness." Her eyes carefully avoided mine as she began to cry again. It was as if she were saying, "Don't spoil it for me; I am trying to get candy by making believe I am unhappy."

The tears were turned on and off like a water faucet. She could laugh as easily as she cried. Thea was believing that if she stopped crying she might not get what she wanted. Her game of unhappiness was her tool. Later that day, Thea, Suzi and I discussed the episode. How ironic and amazing that Thea really had been aware of exactly what she had been doing. She casually informed us, "You know before, when I was crying and everything . . . well, I was really just making believe so you would buy me candy."

In addition to using unhappiness as a tool (as Thea had), many of us also tend to use unhappiness as a gauge to measure the degree of our desires or even loving. The more miserable we feel when we do not get what we want or when we lose something we love, then the more we believe we cared. The converse might be: if we were not unhappy about not getting something or losing it, then maybe we did not want it enough. And even more fearful might be the belief that if we allowed ourselves to be happy under most or all circumstances, then we might, thereafter, not want anything or care about anyone. If we were perfectly satisfied with our situation, we might not move toward new opportunities. We also might fear that we would be cold, insensitive and unfeeling if we weren't unhappy in many situations.

I think that my biggest fear was that if I did become perfectly happy, I might stop moving. But, as I became more content with myself, I found the opposite to be true. It was easier to want more and try to accomplish more because, in many instances, my feeling good was no longer at stake. Whether I got what I wanted or not, I could still be comfortable. And yet, in permitting myself to freely want more, I noticed myself getting more of what I wanted.

*   *   *

The key to what we could and might choose to do with our son, Raun, would be grounded in our beliefs. Understanding the dynamics of those beliefs and digesting the beauty of that awareness would facilitate our comfort and willingness to view our son clearly, to trust our decisions and pursue our wants.

Each belief lies atop a mountain of beliefs. And unhappiness, which is the experience of certain kinds of beliefs, is based on a logical system of reasoning. Those reasons or beliefs are therefore available for investigation. Unveil the system of beliefs and therein lies the possibility of discarding the short-circuit of unhappiness. Pull the plugs on those self-defeating concepts and the "Attitude" will evolve. Buddha once said, "Remove the suffering and you get happiness." It is what remains when we have worked through the misery, the discomforts and the fears. It is what we find beneath the debris of bad feelings and unsettling visions.

An opened doorway loomed before me . . . beckoning with its intrigue. More than just a tool or technique to solve problems. The Option Method: philosophical, but not just a philosophy; therapeutic, but not just a therapy; educational, but not just an education. A willingness to accept in order to see. To want in order to get. To become in order to just be.

You create yourself again if you want to.

Different and original. Not only a dynamic, beautiful and free-flowing investigation into self-defeating attitudes and crippling beliefs, but it was the beginning of a new perspective. I no longer had to accept half measures. I knew that I could choose to believe or not to believe anything that I wanted to . . . that I was the mover and the ultimate interpreter.

Unlike other disciplines (Freudian, Gestalt, Behaviorism, Primal, Encounter, etc.), the Option Method was not a painful or divine pursuit in which only the therapist or teacher knows the right answer for sure. Not a treatment or a miracle, Option maintained an infinite respect for the student or client. No longer waiting in an office for someone else to give you the message . . . to tell you about yourself and make judgments. I knew it to be a joyful pursuit into myself . . . to uncover, discover

26

and re-create. An adventure in which you are the expert. You rechoose old beliefs or create new ones. Emancipating. A virgin landscape upon which I walked and found new ways to be with myself.

Once a close friend told me his cousin had just died. I asked him immediately how close he was to the deceased since it was not obvious. It was as if I asked to know how bad I should feel. If my friend had told me that the relationship was close and valued, I might have cried with him or shared his grief. If the relationship was described as distant and unpleasant, then I would know to treat it casually. I searched for my response. I could choose my degree of unhappiness or happiness or neutrality based on what I believed to be appropriate to the situation. With that type of awareness and many others, I could now explore my beliefs and reasons for unhappiness in other situations and decide whether or not to modify them or discard them as the basis of my feelings and my behavior.

I realized that going to work and making a living was not a "must" or a "should," but something I really wanted. I began to look beneath the discomforts and understood that in believing that work was a "must" I had never allowed myself the freedom to enjoy it. Touching on all my beliefs about anxiety and tension which I thought was a necessity in order to achieve success. Working through all the "good" reasons I believed I had for feeling deprived . . . rejecting so many self-defeating concepts about needing things and about making myself unhappy if I didn't get them. A considered and studied liberation.

It was like having wings. Soaring. Opening doors that I had never believed existed. Suzi and I evolved into a new way of being, discarding much of the old unhappiness by continually investigating our beliefs and making new choices. Three and a half years of redesigning our lives, teaching and counseling others. Communicating. Expanding our private and group experiences by working with and supervising other students. Building a more loving foundation with the bricks and mortar of a new attitude that grew from week to week. We were alive and planting more seeds. Passing it on was something we knew to do.

We were allowing ourselves to enjoy more and to want more. Suzi and I found a new basis for our relationship and marriage.

27

We no longer exchanged comments like "If you loved me, you would do this or that." Each of us grew happier being with each other. We took our togetherness and stripped it of all the elaborate expectations and conditions. We thereby eradicated many of the disappointments and conflicts and were more permissive with each other, more accepting. And this flowed over to Bryn and Thea. Being more sensitized to the beliefs that we "sell" them each and every day, we became more tolerant of what they were wanting and more appreciative of their individuality. It was these attitudes that constituted a firm foundation for ourselves and formed the springboard from which we developed our entire approach with Raun.

*   *   *

All the decisions we made, our comforts and discomforts, our concerns and confusions, the exploration of ourselves and our family, and the pursuit of Raun begins here . . . with our beliefs.

What was the question for us? Was there ever any other than our wanting to be happy? Yes, we had called it by other names —comfort, peace, popularity, excitement, success, money, and so on. And, yes, we had camouflaged it with other categories and goals we considered important.

The Freudian might have called for adaptation and adjustment. The Gestaltist for awareness and being in touch. The Humanists push for self-actualization. But why? What is it that we chase with such haste and fascination? Isn't it all just our wanting to be happy . . . to feel good with ourselves and those around us? And if that is where we want to go, why wait? Can't we have it now? For us, for Raun . . . be happy now while we still continued to pursue our wants and clarify our directions. Indeed, wouldn't our coming from happiness instead of anger or guilt or fear or anxiety probably increase our effectiveness with our son and with what we might be wanting for him?

We could see that if we were not confused or diverted by fears about Raun, we would be able to see him more clearly . . . better for him and more functional for us.

I have heard it said that there are no stupid men on the face of the earth, just unhappy ones. Fearing to see too much or too little. Afraid to allow themselves the freedom to want and not to get. Concerned with the judgments of others or their own recriminations. All these considerations before taking their first step. A happy man, unencumbered by anxiety or fear, can allow himself to absorb everything—so that when he decides to act, he does so with the maximum information available. He understands that the more he knows the better equipped he is. He can allow himself the freedom not to worry about his future . . . the freedom to be okay with himself whether he wins or loses. The freedom to succeed. The freedom to fail and be content.

Does it sound too easy? Like some inexplicable daydream . . . the pop fantasy of a contemporary Wizard of Oz. The question to ask is, "Do we freely choose our beliefs or are they cast into the cement of our genetic structure?" Are they understandable or mysterious, lost in some unknowable unconscious? Is our son confined by some irreversible malady or could he be a fountain of new inspirations? What determines what we feel about him . . . whether we feel good or bad, whether we are happy or unhappy with him? What is the genesis of our feelings? Is our particular vision of our son the direct result of a medical-psychiatric vision of mental health or the result of our own beliefs and attitudes? Do we learn to be unhappy, fearful, anxious, angry, etc. or is there an unhappiness virus? Could we be perfectly happy about Raun as he is, if we chose to be?

One Friday afternoon, Bryn came home after spending the day at a friend's house. She wanted to talk. She had overheard a conversation between her friend's mother and another woman. My daughter was distressed and confused.

"Daddy, what did Dana's mother mean when she called Raun a 'tragedy'?" She looked up at me with unusual softness and concentration. Although it was apparent that she knew what the word meant, she did not fully understand all the subtle and far-reaching ramifications. She had, in fact, intuitively grasped the tone and attitude that was probably implicit in that conversation.

"Bryn, when someone believes that what happens or the way something is, is bad or terrible, they call it a tragedy. It is their way of describing something they would feel miserable and sad about if it ever happened to them. I guess because Raun is different and behaves differently than other children, they

29

were thinking that was bad. Do you think that it's bad or sad that your brother is different?"

"Oh no, Daddy. I love Raun. I would like to be able to play with him the way my friends can play with their little brothers and sisters. But that's okay; he's so cute and funny, Daddy."

The beliefs and fears of others had created a tide of commentary about this delicate little boy that had filtered through to our children. Whispers and innuendos. And what about their vision of tragedy? Was it just a word to label the feelings they had after judging a situation as bad? Perhaps. But, perhaps, even more than that. Unfortunately, many of us are never fully aware that these beliefs embody judgments sometimes so potent that they become self-fulfilling prophecies.

Perhaps the following example can illustrate in gross simplification how diverse our beliefs can be about the very same occurrence, and how they affect our reactions and feelings. A girl stands on the steps of a train about to leave for college for the first time. On the platform is her family. Her father is very proud and is feeling good that his daughter has grown into such an independent young woman now going off to school. But he is also feeling bad about believing he will be lonely and miss her. The mother is sobbing and quite overwhelmed with her sense of loss and the passage of time. The girl's little sister is feeling joyful and elated knowing that she will inherit her sister's room and become a more important part of her family simply by default. Just at that moment, a stranger walks past observing the entire situation. He has absolutely no feelings about the matter. Involved in the same experience, each person reacts in accordance with their beliefs. The father believes the situation to be both good and bad, the mother judges it to be bad and the sister judges it to be good for her. The stranger made no judgment. He was not involved and therefore did not activate a belief about the situation; thus, he developed no feelings about the event.

What we feel and how we act are dependent on our beliefs, which are freely chosen. We are continually accepting and adopting beliefs of parents, peer groups, teachers, magazines, television, governments, religions and our culture. No act, event or person is intrinsically good or bad . . . we call it what we will; we define it, love it, hate it, embrace it, reject it and

30

become unhappy or happy about it according to what we believe. And there is no difference between a belief we acquired in childhood and one we adopted just yesterday. As long as we continually and actively believe it, we give it power today.

Yet, if my beliefs are ones that I can choose, if I can be the expert in understanding my own dynamic, then I can uncover, discover and recreate if I want to. I can choose old beliefs, the beliefs of others or create new ones.

If we are unhappy about Raun, it is because we have corresponding beliefs or judgements. It means that we believe a child like Raun is bad for us, for himself and for others. Our unhappiness about him or any other child who does not meet our standards of behavior or acceptability can result in punitive and disapproving action on our part. In the extreme, with an autistic child, a short-circuit situation develops. Because the child does not behave "normally," he is discarded behind walls of cold and numb institutions. His existence is considered a burden. Often, these children were said to be the cause of unhappiness in others. Many families and parents crumble under the pressure of their own guilt and despair in the face of these conclusions.

Couldn't we be happy about Raun right now without having any answers, without solving problems of his behavior and our relationship to him? Why should we need Raun to act or perform in certain ways before we would allow ourselves to feel good about him and ourselves? Why do we have to believe something must change in a favorable direction in order for us to be joyful about our son? Why do we often make happiness a reward, the bonus we allow ourselves to feel after we get what we want or as the result of doing something we believe is good?

I am not suggesting that unhappiness is bad. Nor am I implying that anyone should or must be happy or that everyone even cares to be happy, but for those of us who want to feel good, these are the questions.

Many of our discomforts and bad feelings are an outgrowth of our systems of beliefs. Unhappiness is an acceptable, if not applauded, reaction to many situations judged to be bad for the individual or the fabric of our communities. As a device, it is used to motivate, to stay in touch and to measure our commitments. Unfortunately, this often results in a short-circuiting

31

which causes the pains, the ulcers, the high blood pressure, the anger, the violence, the divorces, the frustrations and the anxieties. These by-products far exceed the effectiveness of the mechanism and take an incredible toll on most of us.

Our antidote was the Attitude. Creating more than a process, it had become an integral part of our life style.

* * *

We were still in the initial stages of reckoning with our dilemma and dealing with Raun. Our decision to intervene ourselves was developing, yet still pristine. Make contact . . . make it significant. We wanted to touch our son and have him know us.

We felt that our ability to perceive Raun clearly and our capacity to create an effective program were dependent upon our being comfortable with ourselves and therefore the situations with our child. Suzi and I. Endless hours exploring with each other our fears and anxieties. Everything we were experiencing. Belching up the bile of guilt. The verbal bleeding. Not wanting the pain . . . and yet we continued to try to clear our vision, to move through the fog of despair.

Questions. Probing. After-dinner conversations flowing into the bedroom. Lying awake together and talking. Looking out the sliding glass doors and catching a glimpse of the sky. The moonlight infiltrating the room and lighting the ceiling. Highlights of a Daliesque painting that one of our friends designed and another friend painted on the bedroom ceiling. An abstract perspective of geometric forms with its huge spoon positioned to hang just above my head. Filling my eyes with it while my ears were soaked with our explorations. What about institutionalization? What about responsibility? What about the fears and disappointments?

Evenings passed into the early-morning hours. Eyelids drooped over half-covered pupils. A darkness settled below our eyes. We drifted off to sleep only to reawaken in the morning continuing to talk as if there had been no interruption . . . no sleep.

There was the psychoanalytical theory of the cold and hostile environment. Remember that first year with Raun. We were

32

with him. We did love him. Saying it aloud to each other. Hearing it and knowing that it was true. We were with him as we were with the girls. Remembering our first reactions to his withdrawals, which we had never seen as moving away. We had believed that he was developing an early independence. We were proud of his fortitude and excited about his strength. Who knew then it was just the beginning . . . like sand drifting through our fingers. More than accepting, we did not want to push him, to close him in. In his vacant slide over a period of four months, we had allowed it. Maybe even contributed? Possible, but it did not seem to be so.

And the pediatrician who said that he would outgrow it. Feeling skittish about that shortsighted judgment, but buying it anyway . . . and the delay until we continued to move on. Asking more questions and not being satisfied.

Suzi sitting on the grass. Another evening in the warm, still air. Reviewing for me her intimate conversations with God. Pregnant with Raun and forgetting to ask that he be healthy. While carrying the girls, that had been her only request. This time she had opted for another priority . . . "please make it a boy." Always assuming it would be a healthy child. Superstitious behavior? Perhaps. But important now because it irked her, haunted her . . . did she make the omission that caused the flaw? And, indeed, was it a flaw? Back and forth as the dew began to settle on our skin. Slamming the ideas and discomforts across some invisible net until each of us could field the other's serve.

Thinking of Raun, his little face looking out through the bars of the crib. What about my interactions with him? My participation? I had given each child similar amounts of time and involvement when they were infants. Maybe I could have given more. Maybe I could have made the difference. And yet, after investigating my beliefs beneath the fear, I found that my anxiety had stemmed from the following thought: time involvement might be more important than quality involvement. Since I knew this was not so, I discarded it and moved on.

Did the doctor overdose Raun with antibiotics during his bout with the ear infection? Did that cause brain damage? Could this be the result of severe dehydration during infancy? Had we been lax in choosing a physician? Foolish in allowing him to prescribe medication without interfering? Had we accepted the theory of hearing deficiency to keep the truth at a safe distance? We sweated and worked through each idea. Exhausted.

Bait each other into saying whatever we could think of that was negative or bad. Throw it all on the table. If it is a housecleaning of our feelings, go all the way. Fertilize the unhappiness. Get it out. Deal with it so we could be free. Playing devil's advocate for each other . . . a confrontation with the phantoms of fear. In the end: tired, but freer; worn, but alive with desire. It was ours and we could make it an adventure.

Summer had just begun. The warm air was heavy. A taste of green and the scent of fertile earth. We grabbed the girls for a weekend on Shelter Island, leaving behind all the projects Suzi and I worked on together for my business. Raun stayed with Nancy . . . a seventeen-year-old girl who, over the past five years, had become so close to all of us that we considered her part of our family.

We wanted to share ourselves and our feelings with Bryn and Thea. To be with them, help them with us, with Raun. Bryn had tried continuously to make contact with her brother. Often, she accepted his lack of interest . . . but, more and more, she became frustrated and melancholy over his rejections. Just before this weekend, she became extremely upset after yet another refusal.

Round-table discussions. Even Thea, now just five years of age, was a concerned participant and peer in our little group.

"Daddy," said Bryn, "maybe Raun really doesn't like me; maybe there is something wrong with me and he doesn't want to be with me."

"Okay," I answered, "could you imagine Raun sometimes not answering you because he didn't hear you? Suppose he was deaf, would you be angry if he didn't look at you when you called?"

"Of course not, Daddy."

"Good," I replied. "We don't know why your brother is the way he is. Many doctors who have seen him call what he does autistic behavior . . . which simply means there is a name for the kind of thing that Raun does. Maybe Raun can't help himself right now. For some reason, it's hard for him to look at us or play with us . . . he is really doing the best he can. So, when you call him and he doesn't answer, it just means that he can't respond or doesn't know how to respond. It has nothing to do with you or with his loving and caring about you." Tears began to stream down Bryn's cheeks . . . there was no anger or frustration in her expression. But, there was the dawning of a new realization. Suzi held her close while I stroked her hair. I held Thea's hand tightly as her eyes glazed over.

The next morning the hot sun baked our bodies on the sand. The light danced on the surface of the water. We shared tuna sandwiches and warm Coke and enjoyed each other. Bryn and Thea dared the soft surf with their toes, laughing and giggling. Sometimes they found time or interest to gesture or wave in our direction.

Thea had not really discussed her feelings. We were aware that her relationship with Raun was less problematic. Thea was the family Gauguin and a worshiper of privacy. She had little trouble with Raun's apparent desire to be alone. If he did not heed her beckoning, she would play beside him in the same room. Willing to be by him, not needing him to participate.

Yet Suzi continued to probe Thea gently. After two hundred staccato intros, she made the first statement. Thea noted Raun was getting more and more attention. The weights on the scale seemed to have changed. Notes of jealousy. We reviewed with her the reasons . . . all having nothing to do with our caring about her, our loving her. She smiled sheepishly. That was what she was testing . . . looking for the reconfirmation.

The last evening we borrowed a motorcycle. Suzi and I cruised the perimeter of this small and quaint island. Thoughts of other times, the first years of our marriage. Riding another cycle over the mountains of Vermont into Canada. Dinners at roadside stands . . . the curbs our seats, the streets our table. Saving up pennies each week to buy cigarettes as I played out the contemporary dilemma of a struggling young writer as Suzi supported both of us.

The air against our faces now a fast and accelerating massage. Suzi locked her hands around my waist. I leaned the machine into a turn and banked with the curve of the road. I could feel her begin to cry. We stopped and walked along the water. She was letting the rest of it go. Diamond-like headlights from the sky glared across the water and danced on the tears gliding down Suzi's face.

Sunday night, back at home. Settling into the style of our lives and putting our hands to the wheel.

We had recalled all the notations and diagnostic concepts. Reviewed all the articulated theories and procedures. We heard all the professionals give their talks about hopelessness and limited futures. Even our family doctor looked listlessly at the floor and shook his head from side to side upon learning about the diagnosis. We saw other parents of similar children. We heard their outcries and accusations . . . their anguish, their guilt and their searching. Saw their failure to receive any help or meaningful advice. All the traditional, negative beliefs . . . all the visions of exhaustion and hopelessness. The giving up. The half-hearted starts. The inevitable and tragic institutionalizations.

We queried the Option man about our dilemma, and even he suggested that we leave Raun alone. He thought that if he could, or wanted to, Raun would come to us. We disagreed. We did not believe that Raun had the receptive apparatus or conceptual capabilities to decide whether he wanted to join our world or not. We knew there was more that we could do. There was more that we wanted to do. Why couldn't there be an Option Method of reaching and educating children like Raun?

All alone. Suzi and I. Holding it together. What did we know about our son? Distant and encapsulated . . . yes. But he was also gentle, soft and beautiful, happy with himself and the fantasies of his universe. Quiet and peaceful with an incredible talent for concentration on objects. Raun was a flower, not a weed. A journey, not a burden. Perhaps a gift, but certainly not an affliction. We would intervene.

We decided we could have special and different wants for Raun, but that our relationship with him would not be conditional upon them. To be happy and not judgmental . . . this would be the place to begin with Raun. Although this had been our attitude, our reaffirming it, our verbalizing it helped us to be more aware of the specialness that was to characterize our dealing with our "special" son.

36

We would kiss the earth that the literature had cursed. We would embrace all the beauty of our son. Raun would become for us a beautiful and enriching journey into our own humanity. We would walk together.

Three

No conditions. No expectations. No judgments. This attitude would be the place to begin with Raun. We would continually dedicate ourselves to this vision of acceptance and approval. We decided that his "isms" (the ritual behavior of rocking, spinning, finger flapping and so on) were perfectly okay with us. In fact, as a result of our initial observations, we sensed that his "isms" were tools that he used to help him make sense out of a complex and bizarre confusion of perceptions. Perhaps they were his healthy way of coping . . . never meaning to make a comment on us or the environment. Even the excessive mouthing and drooling, the hours spent examining his fingers, the compulsion for sameness . . . perhaps they were all just adaptive processes of his dysfunctioning system in its attempt to meet and digest an unpredictable world.

First we must know him completely. We decided on marathon sessions of observation. Suzi and I spent endless hours sitting with Raun and observing him. In the mornings, we were with him as he sat on the kitchen table with the light dancing through the picture window and bouncing off his rocking form. We walked around him, catching his silhouette against the stained-glass window we had built into the wall. Its New England ecclesiastical imagery formed a muted background for his ritual. Afternoons were spent outside, with Raun sitting between us in the woods behind our house. The one-hundred-year-old oak trees created an umbrella, shielding us from the summer sun.

We watched him as he rocked his body and spun every round object he could find. We started to imitate him . . . for him, but also for us. Through our doing and repeating his behavior, we hoped to find some relevant insight or understanding. We also believed that this was one of the few channels open to us through which we could let him know that we were with him. We wanted to use his cues as a basis of communicating.

Evenings in the den with Raun in the middle of a multicolored Navajo rug, setting his plate spinning across the intricate geometric patterns of tightly-woven fibers. He never once looked up . . . to see us or the paintings hanging on the walls which were created by his mother. He never glanced out the windows to catch the fleeting image of the sky or the trees set into motion by the wind. He never departed from his circle of activity.

We initiated a very elaborate imitation format that extended beyond our periods of observation. When Raun spun plates for hours at a time in a room, Suzi and I and whoever else was in the house would gather up plates and pans and spin beside him. Sometimes there would be as many as seven of us spinning with him, turning his isms into an acceptable, joyful and communal event. It was our way of being with him . . . of somehow illustrating to him that he was okay, that we loved him, that we cared and that we accepted him wherever he was.

This was in direct contrast to one of the more recently developed techniques for dealing with these children which was coming into vogue. It is called behavior modification. Thus far, it has had only limited success. Nevertheless, more and more professionals are using it as a total approach. Although we believed that, in part, it was a useful educational tool (which at times we employed), its essential premises and philosophy made it a very strange and questionable method to be used as a base for an entire program. The behaviorist, at the outset, makes many judgments about an autistic or deviant child and his behavior. Some activities are categorized and labeled as "bad" or undesirable while others are deemed good. The underlying reasons for the behavior would not be considered applicable in treatment. Only what was concretely observable would be dealt with. So, if the "isms" were undesirable, then they would be extinguished through an elaborate system of rewards and punishments.

What is not considered is the dignity of the child . . . his right to be who he is and how he is. What is not considered is the message of the child and the tone of his statement. If just part of a program starts with disapproval, even if only implicit . . . if the statement is that these little people are bad and their behavior is somehow wrong, what then can possibly be the eventuality? When you push someone, there is an almost automatic tendency to push back. You are saying to the child that he "must" or "should" be with you in a way that you define as acceptable. Why would anyone want to be with someone who is disapproving of him? How could one want to learn from someone who does not allow him any freedom or prerogative in the process? Why ignore what the child wants?

We believed that telling Raun, in whatever way we could, that he was accepted and approved of was the first and most important part of our journey. We were aware that the fruits of any labor would be thin if we pushed or pulled him. If we were to intervene in his world, it would have to be *with* him, with his allowing; it would have to be consistent with his wanting. We believed his behavior was the best that he could do, and if we wanted him to do more, we would first have to facilitate his wanting more. Help him. Show him. Love him.

More days of observing. Suzi and I sat on the floor in the den, Raun on the other side. At first rocking, then spinning. There was something so well defined about his movements . . . nothing seemed arbitrary. It was as if we were looking into the dynamics of an entire universe. A little boy lost in the complexity of his self-stimulating activities. We noted his mood. Really happy. Although the literature, at least an overwhelming percentage of it, defined autism as an emotional and psychotic condition, Raun did not seem to fit the mold. Autistic yes. Psychotic no.

What I had read seemed disconnected. Some authorities defined the "isms" as symptoms; items not to be dealt with but merely discarded as the arbitrary topping of underlying feelings. Others saw them as definite statements being made by the child as a protest or disapproval of his world. I wondered if anyone sitting with a child like this with no preconceived notions or judgments could ever come up with such hypotheses. What Raun did he did all the time . . . whether in our presence or alone. His movements were exacting. They were also comforting and consoling to him. Only for isolated and fleeting moments did he venture outside himself and dare to make contact. Each time he did, he seemed to do it with great difficulty. It was our growing awareness of the constructive and exciting nature of his behavior patterns that would help us penetrate his universe.

Traditionally, the autistic child is not properly diagnosed until the age of three or four years old. Some parents do not become activated until their child is older and his behavior more obviously deviant. Others resist recognition because of their own fears or anxieties. Still others seek early consultation, only to be confronted by pediatricians and professionals who adopt a wait-and-see attitude. Once the child has been functionally autistic for years, their fantastic array of special behavior patterns are usually intermixed with a good deal of anger and pain. Perhaps what has often been considered the cause of autism is merely the eventual result.

If these children cannot put the world together in a functional or meaningful way, but are forced to participate in an environment where "putting the world together" is expected and stressed, then their deficiencies, conjoined with this pressure, might easily create anxieties and fears. Continued without relief or interruption, their emotional problems could escalate until the unhappiness grows so acute and pervasive that their behavior and attitudes reflect it, becoming so strange and unacceptable that they are then labeled schizophrenic.

In contrast, Raun at seventeen months old was tranquil and comfortable in terms of moods and feelings. He was not living in a situation of pressure and disapproval. And, although his autistic behavior was rampant, the patterns were fairly new. Not an angry or anxious little boy, but happy and content. There was no reason to assume that his functional deviance was born out of emotional trauma and stress. No reason to define the genesis of his malady as a response to his own feelings.

41

Every morning, standing in his crib, he stared into the looking glass of himself . . . eyes sparkling in their porcelainlike
setting, he was a vision of lucidity as the breeze moved gently
through his curly hair and bathed his face in its coolness. And
when Suzi changed his diapers or washed his face, he accepted
the distraction passively, looking fleetingly at her, then returning to his private universe. The soft white talcum powder
melted unobtrusively into his skin. Brain-blessed. It was now
that we would be able to reach him most effectively . . . that we
could love him and touch him in a meaningful and lasting manner.

On the tops of tables, sitting on the tile floor, rocking on the
rug, spinning outside on the cement walk, we were with him
participating and observing. From early morning to early evening we stayed with him continually until he went to sleep.
Skipping meals or having them on the floor next to him, we
made every second count. We took notes and wrote down questions. The hours became days. The days became weeks. We
tried to know him as if we were inside him. We found our love
increased with each passing week as we grew infinitely more
respectful of his dignity and specialness.

It was during the second week of our marathon observation
period. Watching him for hours spinning on the kitchen floor,
every round object being set into motion. Dishes. Tops and
plates. Pans and balls. This one time, he came upon a rectangu-
lar shoebox. He picked it off the floor and held it in his hands
for almost twenty-five minutes. He did not move . . . just occasionally stroked it, touching the cardboard with his fingers while
moving his eyes along its edges. Then, quite suddenly, he put
the tip of one of the corners of the box on the floor, balanced
it with his left hand and set it into motion with his right. No trial
and error. He had actually used his mind analytically and with
great sophistication in order to get what he had wanted. Before
he moved or made a single test, he had analyzed the potential
of the box as a spinning object and then synthesized a method
to achieve it. Still only seventeen months old. Incredible. Amazing and slick. A significant piece of behavior hinting at the vast
field of intelligence that we felt existed beneath the surface of
his bizarre patterns.

And what of the fundamental symptom most characteristic of

autistic children? What of their fascination with inanimate objects while ignoring the world of people and social interaction? Thinking of Raun still on the floor. When he was not self-stimulating, he might stare for ten or twenty minutes at a time. A sphinx surveying the awesome pyramid of reality while transfixed in time and space.

Now Raun was fixating on the base of the dining-room table, which was richly ornamented with antique scrollwork. His eyes became glued to it. And this object of his interest did not move. It did not emit sounds. The base would only move if someone moved it and that was highly unlikely. Therefore, in its inertia, this inanimate metal base was highly predictable. Secure. He could deal with objects that were stationary or, like the cups he spun, he would involve himself in a limited selection of items that he could absolutely control for his very own special purposes.

In contrast, when people entered the room, they were usually moving. Erratic. Noisy. Unpredictable and usually uncontrollable. If one of Raun's organic deficits was a problem or deficiency with thinking—a problem of memory and recall—a problem of holding things together in time and space; then surely objects would be easier to deal with than people. If each person entering the room was always a new and unrelated experience to Raun, then each one of us might be a hundred different people to him. What a confusing and perplexing bombardment of data we must create, a diverse spectrum of sporadic images.

To complicate things even more, each time we moved, we did so at a different speed, turned in a different direction and made different sounds. If Raun could not make sense out of us, if we were merely a perplexing jumble of perceptions, then why should he not shut us out? Why shouldn't he prefer the infinitely more peaceful and predictable world of inanimate objects?

He was aloof and separate from people while pouring his energy into objects. Naturally, this dilemma would produce a child who did not relate to or imitate people. Therefore, learning would be severely curtailed and, in some instances, impossible. Language acquisition, which also depends on imitation, would be affected. In addition, communications and manipulating others in the environment would have no meaning in Raun's peopleless world.

In our observation, the assumption that these children do not relate to people because they choose not to is true, but with a major and essential qualification: they hesitate doing those things that are extremely difficult and problematic for them to do. Unfortunately, that often includes most normal behavior patterns and simple tasks. It would be like a person who has an inner-ear balance dysfunction giving up tight-rope walking after trying numerous times and finding it extremely difficult . . . if not impossible. Raun, too, would choose what he could work with—it would require incredible drive or desire to leave the graspable for the unintelligible.

It appeared to us that his process of thinking and perceiving was dysfunctioning. We would find Raun upon waking sitting in his crib, fixating on his hand. He usually concentrated on only one hand—moving it close to his eyes and alternately moving his fingers up and down. At times, the flexing had a rhythm to it. This occurred often throughout the day. Each time his hand came into his visual field, he would stop and visually investigate it. The surveying could take hours. If he were four to eight months old, we might consider this normal and appropriate . . . a child discovering his limbs. But what did it mean if one year later than the norm the child still seemed to be discovering those same limbs? Every time he saw his hands, it was as if he saw them for the first time. Then, naturally, it was a source of endless contemplation. Each time was a new and disconnected experience, unrelated to his past, to his memory or the utilization of it.

He was cemented to each experience with no capacity to draw upon a previous situation or understanding. If he couldn't put it together, of course he might spend hours or days, or even years, going over the same experience. And then, obviously, he would have no time to learn new things. Limited and ultimately retarded. And yet . . .

We continually tried an experiment with Raun: We could establish good eye contact with Raun by getting him to focus on a cookie . . . we would bring it in front of his eyes, let him fixate on it and then move it slowly so that he could track it. Suzi would then hold up a piece of paper and I would bring the

44

cookie behind it. Raun would follow until he lost visual contact with the cookie. Then he would remain fixed on the last place he had seen it. He would stare confused into empty space, lingering for a period of time, and then turn away. Even if we carefully showed him that the cookie was behind the paper, once the paper blocked his vision, he would lose contact and become disoriented.

According to Piaget, the average eight-month-old child has developed the intellectual maturity and skill to sustain images in his mind even if the objects envisioned are out of view. In most cases, the eight-month-old will pursue the hidden object. Raun, at seventeen months, could not retain the object in his mind without seeing it, and he never pursued it. When it disappeared from his vision, it disappeared from his mind and the face of the earth.

A variation on the same theme: Raun's most consistent interest, besides his "isms," was certain foods. Yet he never asked for or cried for food; in fact, he never expressed any wants. If he was not fed, he made no protest or plea. But, when food was put before him, he did know it was something he could eat and he would eat it if he was hungry. Perhaps Raun did not call for food because he did not know how. Nevertheless, when soft baby food (the only kind of food he could eat without choking) was introduced to him, he would always eat with some apparent interest. When he finished, no matter how much or how little he ate, he never called for more.

Each time he was fed, it was again just another new and disconnected experience. So, although his internal system registered hunger, his intellect could not connect with the remembered remedy. It would be as if he forgot each time that it was food that satisfied his hunger. He would not do anything to get food because, for him, there would be nothing he knew to do. His environment had no meaning for him in most instances.

And what of the spinning and the rocking? Possibly they were a way to soothe the bombardment of input and sensory experience. As Raun leaned over the objects he set into motion, he would rock as if one with them. His hands and fingers responded with erratic and jerky patterns of movement. Could Raun be living in a world that always turned? Could his early ear infection have disrupted the proper development and operation of his inner ear? Was he always in a state of dizziness? Although he learned to walk when he was a year old and his movements were steady, often he walked on his toes. Was this his way of trying to establish better balance? Perhaps he spun to make the world catch up to his way of perceiving it. In effect, he would be making the world stand still.

These self-stimulating activities, which he controlled, also had their own built-in sensory feedback. In many ways, it is no different from a person humming to himself or rocking in a rocking chair or snapping his fingers continuously to music. These too are self-stimulating behaviors, with the important distinction that they are socially acceptable and are usually not kept up in "apparent" excess. The questions. The unanswerable questions.

Audio insensitivity and staring. A little boy who could see, but appeared blind, who could hear, but appeared deaf. Suzi would call to him and he would not respond. Once, I slammed a book on a table no more than a foot from his head. He did not seem to hear it; he did not blink or move. Yet, at times, low music coming from another room could grab his attention. Inconsistent. The same held true for his vision. Staring and blind to some objects, yet curiously alert and attentive to others. One morning I moved my open hand quickly in front of his eyes; he did not even blink. All the sensory intake systems were intact, yet he could turn off his sight or hearing at will. Extraordinary . . . to be able to cut off perceptions that were being absorbed by his senses. Why?

Perhaps there were no simple attainable answers but there was enough evidence to form an hypothesis. It might be that he was overbombarded or oversensitive to his perceptions. Thus he could stop reception as a form of self-protection. But perhaps the opposite was true: He could have a low-volume intake system, and, therefore, he cut one sense off so that he could heighten or concentrate on another. While he was looking at something, he cut off his hearing so as not to be distracted. Sometimes, while he was listening, his eyes were vacant. A regulatory problem in which he simplified input for easier digestion? And then, sometimes, there seemed to be a third possibility—that the replay system in his mind was so vibrant and active he stopped perceiving in order to watch his own

46

internal picture show. Maybe it was a combination of all these factors. Our task was to keep alert . . . be responsive and help him regulate his contact with the sensory world.

The question was of perception and the problem was recognition, retention and recall. Raun lacked the full power of thinking. A cognitive problem . . . an inability to match the new data with the old . . . an inability to generalize from one experience to the next. He could not form a coherent entity out of his experiences. The magic was not there. No organized whole, just fragmented pieces. It was as if he maintained a primitive expectation of help, but never thought to seek it from any source . . . maybe also unaware of what he was seeking until it arrived in his view.

Raun Kahlil, confined to the now of his senses. We knew that, ultimately, language development would be crucial in helping him catalog his intake and go from the concrete to the abstract. Language would be his wings.

We, ourselves, had realized a new clarity, an exciting outline being formulated from our being with Raun. Our plunge into his world had had a dramatic impact on us—it was like exploring a new frontier, the deep probing and discovery of a human being. Through our lovely and serene little boy we had been reawakened to the complexities of perceiving and thinking. Whether the origin of his problems began during his hospital stay or stemmed from brain damage, as one physician had suggested, the initial cause was no longer important or significant. We were beginning to come to grips with his world . . . without fear and anxiety, but with love and acceptance and permissiveness. So many things about him had begun to make sense. We no longer faced a stone wall of confusion, but an approachable individual with special problems . . . a living, breathing and beautiful person who had never made any outrageous requests or demands . . . who simply was.

With each passing day, we came to know our son more and more, to know also about the labels, the inferences, the prophecies and confusions. Indeed, there were professionals who in their way were trying to say something, trying to do something, but who were constrained by their own limiting theories and dogma. Even now, they continued to have difficulty analyzing and synthesizing an approach for themselves, for their "pa-

47

tients" and for the distressed parents. Two generations of research and energy had produced elaborate systems of judgments and predictions. And yet, for all this effort, little had transpired that was meaningful for this small boy and others like him. We knew the way would have to come from him and that we could only facilitate and help.

Raun did not need another doctor or interviewer . . . he needed a guide, a teacher, a therapist. "Therapon," the Greek genesis of the word therapist, the essence of which means "assistant" or "comrade in a common struggle."

We knew that helping Raun define himself and his wants (perhaps to be with us, perhaps not) would be the only way to help him reconstruct his inoperative or partially-operating systems, so that his perceptions and thought processes could be more useful in dealing with the world and widening his opportunities to choose.

As we solidified our perspective, we knew that it would take many hours of constant work and constant exposure to intervene, to make contact humanistically and to make more data available to him. Stimulation was essential. Even overstimulation. The more he drifted and became encapsulated, the fewer possibilities there would be for him. Until he could take hold of the world by himself, we would be there each and every moment feeding it to him, redefining it for him, chopping it into digestible parts, breaking it into sections and fragments to be reassembled in the interior of his mind. We knew that now was the time, while he was young. Now while he was supple and developing. Now while he lived the most fertile days of his life. Do it before Raun was sucked away into the rusted walls of time and lost behind an impenetrable barrier . . . wandering alone in the recesses of his head and searching for a passageway that would never be there.

But we did not want just to train him or robotize him or use force or the threat of punishment as others before us had tried to do rather unsuccessfully with other little children like Raun. We wanted to draw out the sap. To fertilize the seed. To watch it flower and bear fruit. Allow him to be and discover his own enriching garden. We wanted to help him reach the limits of his own possibilities, not impose on him standards from outside.

Four

We were now ready to institute a three-phased program. The first part, already in effect, had to do with the attitude of approval and acceptance which would underlie every attempted contact, every approach, every movement we made toward him.

The second phase would be a motivational/therapy experience. Show Raun that our world was beautiful and exciting. Show him that it might be worth his extra effort to depart from his ritualized arena. We knew that it would require special effort on his part. That he would have to want it. We could only provide the increased awareness and the opportunities for him. To venture outside himself into a less-charted and less-predictable world would require extremely strong motivation.

The third phase would be to develop a teaching program of instruction for him by breaking down each activity, each event, into small and digestible parts. We would grossly simplify his external environment in order to let him build new pathways, construct new roads where old ones may have been damaged or broken. For us, autism was a brain or neurological short circuit that created a disorganization in the processing of perceptions and the utilization of memory data. This, in turn, effected an altered state of consciousness and changed patterns of thinking. Raun's current deviances were simply his way of seeing and digesting. We did not want to burden him with having to understand our visions or norms. We did not want to push or pull him and create the serious emotional problems which are so often an outgrowth of autism.

We chose to make contact in an environment with no distractions. Suzi and I decided the optimum room for this was the bathroom, where we could limit interference from audio and visual bombardment. The walls were one-color tile with no paintings or windows. The floor was a simple soft-tone mosaic. With the exception of the three fixtures, the sink, the toilet and the bathtub, the room was quite sparse and unobtrusive. The floor area between the tub and the toilet would be the place to begin. It was approximately four feet by six feet. And, although I would help by working with Raun when I was home in the evenings and on weekends, the sessions would be basically structured and executed by Suzi. Her role in my business, conceiving ideas and copy approaches, would have to be limited. It was the miracle of her excitement, her vivaciousness and her optimism that initiated and permeated our program for our son.

Those first days. Suzi sitting quietly with Raun. Together, but separate. Raun staring at his shoes, then his eyes moving to his hands and finally fixating on the lights in the ceiling. Suzi watching, searching. Hoping for some slight hint of awareness of her existence . . . some ever-so-minute suggestion that he was aware and interested in her presence. His alert eyes seemed like natural mirrors reflecting instead of absorbing or sending information. His porcelain face was inactive . . . the stoic gestures of a priest meditating. From time to time, his delicate little fingers would move aimlessly in the air as if disconnected from the remainder of his body. In this mesmerizing and enclosed presentation of himself, Raun was a towering and awesome figure. A self-contained and self-supporting universe.

Suzi watched as he picked up the plate to spin, holding it ever so carefully on its edge. With great accuracy he twisted his tiny hand and sent the object revolving across the room. Another plate, then another. Raun rose only to retrieve them once they had finished their journeys. He sat again, repeating the pattern and delighting in their movements. Absorbed in the repetitiousness of this activity. Finally he stopped. His eyes crawled over the tiles until they reached the ceiling. They stopped and became fixated on the lights. An endless stare. The fluorescence bathed him with a silhouetted halo. His stillness had the power of the pyramids, ageless, awesome and mysterious. Suzi waited as she looked directly into the lights. After several minutes, her eyes began to tear and the imagery of the ceiling started to go out of focus. But she stayed with it, searching for the meaning in this bleached contemplation.

Finally, he let his eyes fall. He dropped his vision to some vague spot in space directly in front of him. Then he began to rock. Back and forth in an even cadence. He began to hum. Two notes sung in variation and in exact time with each alternative movement. Suzi now moving with him. First she concentrated on empty space. Then she found a spot on the wall and focused on it. As she went forward, the spot became larger; as she rocked backward, the spot became smaller. She moved in the same rhythm as Raun, feeling his body and hers breaking the air in the same thrust. Raun was lost in the motion.

Suzi concentrated on the spot and started to feel slightly fogged. She began to enter his world in a way she found beautiful and enriching. In these movements and in their repetition, there was a hypnotic calm that would come over her, reminiscent of the initial feeling she had gotten when exposed to hypnosis. Soothing and peaceful, it induced a meditative state probably capable of creating alpha waves in the brain—those associated with feelings of well-being. She knew that Raun's way of being had its own rewards . . . an elevation of mood that was often practiced by many religious men in the East. He had designed his own Nirvana.

Her mimicking was not passive or peripheral . . . it was only through her real involvement and her sincere enthusiasm for these activities that she could share the world with Raun and perhaps, in an imperceptible way, communicate her love and approval. She was active, but gentle. Alive, but peaceful.

Whether in the bathroom or outside, Suzi was always willing to bring with her all the objects that Raun would spin and fixate on . . . she wanted him to know that being with her would not be a situation of deprivation. He could have his plates and his pans. He could always have his "isms." The hours became days.

51

Most of the time Raun behaved as if he did not know that Suzi was there. And yet she knew he knew that she was there, that his awareness was increasing each time they were together.

Her aim was to be human, but nonthreatening. Stay quiet and, perhaps, at times be as predictable as an inanimate object. If he was having difficulty in data intake and assimilation, then make yourself easy to digest.

On the eleventh day, after spinning with him for over two hours, Suzi noted his casual sideward glance at her. He was becoming more adventuresome in the bathroom. When he entered, he would now walk quietly around, explore the walls and the fixtures from time to time. Then he would place himself on the floor and stare at the lights. Suzi thought it was time to introduce stimulation, that he was ready and receptive . . . even if only passively receptive.

She moved next to him on the floor so that her thigh was touching him. Slowly she touched his shoulder. Very lightly she stroked his arm. Over and over with an even cadence. Mimicking the rhythm of his rocking. He was alert to her hand. Like an animal allowing what seemed soothing, but attentive to change. Ready to move in an instant. He seemed to be absorbing; then he drifted. Suzi could tell when he was not taking it in . . . yet she continued. He stood up and moved away, staring at the lights again. Suzi stopped, waited about fifteen minutes, then sat down next to him again. She touched his shoulder and then stroked his arm. Again he allowed it and was attentive. Then, again, he drifted. He began to rock; Suzi began to rock.

That evening, we discussed the new responses and activities. We decided that after several hours together Raun seemed to become more responsive. Not that he initiated or sought contact, for he seldom looked at Suzi. But generally he seemed more relaxed, more daring.

Suzi would now have breakfast and lunch with Raun in the bathroom. He liked food. Instead of the isolated and possibly confusing experiences at the table, it would be another vehicle through which to make contact. She would feed him with a spoon, bit by bit . . . never rushing it; in fact, extending the meal by giving him small amounts each time. While he was eating, she would talk softly to him. She would sing and hum.

Through all of this, for those first weeks, he hardly reacted.

Eight or nine hours each day she would sit with him. Feed him. Talk with him. Touch him. Sing to him. Mimic him. Eight or nine hours each day with him oblivious all the time, except for a very few minutes. Precious minutes.

On the weekends, I would sit on the steps outside the bathroom listening to Suzi with Raun in their tiled world. The chatter and the songs alternated with periods of eerie silence. Then Suzi would go into her animal-farm routine. Quacking like a duck. Barking like a dog. Chirping like a bird. Giving the deep and lingering utterances of a cow. She was stepping up the intensity of the stimulation. Raun was now becoming more attentive. The Kaufmans' Theatre of the Absurd. It was like a rehearsal before opening night . . . and the audience was composed of everyone you have ever loved, and each performance had its specialness and significance.

Another discussion on Sunday. Although there was progress, however minor, the major element lacking was eye contact. Without it, we would never be able to move together with Raun. If he did not attend to us, he would only have limited knowledge of us. A sideward glance. Just merely a vague background image captured on the lens of his vision. He would never be able to imitate what he did not see. Since this is a primary and fundamental step in human development and learning, he would not grow. He would have to see more of us in order to grasp more of what there was to know and want. This would be our next major area of concentration.

We would now always feed him at our eye level. Each time we put some food into a spoon, he would attend to it and follow it as it moved. We would bring the spoon to our face and hold it for a few seconds in front of our eyes. As he looked past the food, we would look back at him and smile. Saying "eat" and then giving it to him. This association was critical. Each meal meant about thirty eye contacts . . . thirty opportunities for him to find us through his maze. The progress was immediate. He would now linger on our eyes as if surveying them or investigating their presence. He became more attentive to eating and some of his passivity was lifting.

The third week, Suzi felt that we could now begin to introduce more intervention activities and heighten the stimulation. Expose him to more interaction now that we were able to

have him look at us and follow his food in almost every direction. We did not yet want specifically to teach him, but to
initiate him . . . to bathe him in sensory experiences. We decided to continue using the food as a lure and a reward. Encour-
age him, but allow him to back away. Never force him. Never
plead or push. Never be disapproving when Raun was unavailable and unreachable.

Suzi grew more aggressive in approaching our son. She used
more physical contact—hugging, stroking, tickling, tumbling,
throwing him into the air. She utilized pieces of fruit and pret-
zels as the initial attraction for his involvement in games of
peekaboo and hide-and-seek. She rolled tennis balls between
his legs and put them into his hands. She tried to develop other
games; using water from the sink as a pool to dip his hands into
—cold water, warm water, soapy water. She turned the water
on and off, letting it drip and then surge from the spigot. Everyday activities. A continuum of a program of enrichment and
stimulation. Continual input and exposure. Trying to get
through with more for him to see, hear, feel and internalize. Yet
maintaining care that this was always done with extreme sensitivity to his wanting and allowing it.

Even though he was mute and had no gesture language, it
was becoming evident by some of his reactions that he was
beginning to understand words and expressions. Each activity
and each object was labeled and verbalized. Talking incessantly
was our way of familiarizing him with more humanistic and
social interaction techniques . . . giving a cognitive dimension
to our presence.

Two days each week we would go to the park with Raun.
There, two hundred ducks wallowed in the brown-gray water
of a lyrical man-made lake. The metallic swings, each one
molded into the shape of an animal, glistened in the sunshine.
The tall and short slides. Raun walked beside Suzi mechanically,
vaguely surveying the trees, grass and people, yet uninvolved
and uninterested. Late afternoons Raun floated in our pool,
moving up and down as his body broke the water in playful
rhythms. We pushed him in the hammock. We walked with him
and touched the flowers and leaves to his hands. We tried to
help him those first minutes while he experimented walking
barefoot on the grass. Raun rose on his tiptoes and fell. We

54

helped him to his feet and watched him repeat the procedure. Now we left him to himself. After crawling for a short time, he stood up. This time he moved cautiously as the bottoms of his feet touched the ground.

Suzi mixed earth with water and brought him barefoot into the mud. She watched him wiggle his toes as he smiled in delight. Then his face became fixed and expressionless. Taking his hand, Suzi would go on to games of touching and stroking. Each time he drifted, she would move on unless he pulled against her. When that happened, she would let him be. Every waking hour was filled with contact and experience. Suzi alone put in seventy-five intense and concentrated hours per week with him.

In the evening, while he slept, we discussed his progress. And, although each individual day seemed uneventful, new subtleties continually appeared. He now allowed himself to be held for ten seconds instead of five. On isolated occasions, he would hold my hand or make unexpected eye contact. Smiling when his feet were in the mud was certainly a new kind of response. Suzi was animated and excited. She had found something very personal and meaningful in this dramatic pursuit of her son.

Music was introduced into the sessions. Beethoven and Mahler. Brahms and Bach. Seals and Crofts. Herbie Mann. The Modern Jazz Quartet. Piano concertos by Van Cliburn and the improvisions of Chick Corea. Raun was immediately attentive to the sounds and melodies. Each day, he showed more and more fascination. We had found another special connection into his world. And, with it, a small thrust forward.

One morning, this little noncommunicative and abstract human being came quietly into the bathroom and went directly over to the tape recorder. Although he did not gesture or speak, he turned and looked directly into Suzi's eyes. In the silence and intensity of his glance, she heard him. She jumped up and put the music on immediately. He turned his face to the machine and became lost in the soft serenade. Suzi picked him up into her arms and rocked him back and forth to the tempo of the music.

The food, the music and Suzi's eyes began to have a real and expanded meaning for Raun. Although he persisted in his rocking, spinning and staring, he was becoming mildly involved with people. His looking toward Suzi in front of the tape recorder was his first real, although vague, attempt to communicate with another human being.

We continued to imitate him, trying to be receptive to any cues that he might give us. We wanted to show him that, with minimal efforts, he could move the world outside him, could effect change and control. Show him that he could manipulate people to get more of what he wanted. Show him that wanting was productive.

The imitation was paying off. He would watch us while we were intensely involved. He was doing his "isms" just a bit less. When we sat with him and imitated his behavior, he was now definitely aware of it. And, through that awareness and our involvement, he was attending to us more and more even though a bit tangentially.

Yet he was still dramatically more interested in objects than people. He would still often play in the room as if we did not exist. When we went to pick him up, there were still no anticipatory gestures on his part. In our arms, his body was limp; his arms and legs dangled aimlessly as if he did not know or want to hold on. But there was the fact that now he at least allowed us to hold him for short periods of time before pushing us away. Essentially, he was still solitary, still very self-stimulating.

But the constant contact and stimulation had made a real difference. Our program of intervention was working . . . being with him every minute, facilitating the rebirth of his awareness with touch, sound, food, play, etc. had enabled us to break through. But building this new route was difficult and painfully slow. Raun Kahlil was still content to be alone, and in his aloneness there was still so much distance. And still no prelinguistic language was developing.

Moving on. We found an article in the *New York Times* about the highly-successful experiments with hyperactive and hyperkinetic children in a California hospital utilizing special diets and controlling food intake. The experimentors had discovered that without artificial ingredients and additives in their food, many of these children improved dramatically. Although Raun's problems were certainly very different, there was something in the notations, something between the lines that struck a sympathetic note. We had researched biochemical solutions and megavitamin theories and decided they did not apply. But what about diet? What about his food intake? Suzi and I rummaged through the closets and read all the labels on all our foods . . . artificial this, artificial that, chemical dyes for coloring and additives for food preservation. Unbelievable. Some of the so-called food products contained very little natural food elements. Their labels read like the Who's Who list in chemistry; xunthan gum for consistency, artificial coloring and flavoring, calcium disodium EDTA to preserve freshness, propylene glycol alginate, monosodium glutamate and so on. My stomach belched out its acid as I continued to read the list. All of this we calmly and thoughtlessly consumed. Quick readings of Adelle Davis and others . . . reviewing and surveying a better plan for our and Raun's consumption of food.

Certainly a diet free of these chemicals and artificial additives could only be a plus factor in his life . . . as well as in ours. We did not want to leave any stone unturned. We emptied all the cabinets. We loaded all the nonnatural foods into brown paper bags and distributed them among our friends. And, although we told them what we were doing—and why—they still easily accepted all the unopened bottles and cartons of food. It was an insane and comedic adventure. Our cupboards were almost empty. Our food giveaways had cost at least a hundred dollars. We felt fresh and excited. To the health-food stores with their organically grown vegetables and products free from chemical dyes and preservatives. Buying such unfamiliar items as sesame seeds, soybean oil, Tamari sauce, fresh peanut butter, brown rice, bean sprouts, Hagan-Daz ice cream, sugarless cookies and natural cereals.

Some of the foods tasted strange. Peculiar. We were elated with the feeling that we were making love to our bodies in a special and caring way, that this area of neglect had come into full view and had been dealt with productively. We would try a vegetarian program, substituting fresh fish and high-protein vegetables for meat and meat products. In the end, at least we knew that Raun and all of us would be free of the questionable intake of chemicals and artificial foods.

57

*   *   *

Raun was now more responsive and alert to music, to food, to eye contact. We started to introduce additional materials and teaching games. We bought a large plastic insertion box, in which he could match three-dimensional shapes with appropriate holes. This was to help develop hand-eye coordination and figure-ground perspective. There were red circular shapes, green triangles, blue squares, white diamonds, yellow rectangles and black hexagons. Color differentiation was also a functional aspect of this tool. We brought in wooden building blocks of different sizes and shapes. We found elementary Simplex puzzles which we could use to help him identify shapes and objects. Increasing his small motor coordination, developing his ability to analyze forms, and increasing meaningful interaction with the environment were just some of our goals. The different animals and household items depicted in the puzzles were pieces of reality we wanted to expose him to. All these toys were carefully integrated into the program not as cold and flat objects, but as functions of interpersonal games. Contact, physical as well as communicative, was the fundamental characteristic we were trying to foster. These toys and tools we hoped could become bridges across the valleys of silence.

Sitting on the floor beside Suzi, Raun was withdrawn and aloof. Suzi removed the little cat from its wood slot, held it up to Raun, identified it and then made the sound of a cat. Even her face was furrowed like the animal. Meowing by his face, into his ears, on top of his belly. Then, she lovingly gave the piece to Raun and identified it once again, allowing him the time to investigate it or reject it if he wanted. But he held it, turned it over and surveyed the blank side, exploring its outer edge.

Later, he tried to put the cat back upside down. Suzi rewarded him for approximating the gesture. She gave him some soft cookie (organic) and a hug. Then, taking his tiny fingers, she showed him how to replace the piece. As he tried to duplicate her action, he was again applauded. Finally, after a series of small steps, Raun began to comprehend the procedure. Suzi stroked his hair and spoke softly to him.

58

This activity, as well as all the others in our program, was not simply performed as a mechanical process . . . it was humanized at every level and was a significant vehicle for social interaction. Teaching him specifics at this point was relatively unimportant. Showing him the value and beauty of dealing with others was our primary goal.

As his skill and level of interaction increased, we encouraged Raun to begin and guide his sessions. A selection of toys and games would be placed on the floor before him. He would choose the items to deal with and determine the activity. Go with him. Be sensitive to his wants. Allow him to set the direction and pace the exercises. We responded to his cues and inclination. Rock if he wanted to, do the puzzle if that was what interested him. Feed him if food was chosen. Let him find the energy and the movement from within him.

The first month had passed by swiftly. We had definitely broken through in many areas with our program, although the progress was still embryonic. Raun could now make some eye contact, could accept being touched for short periods of time, could be interested in games, puzzles and music. A growing involvement with people was glimpsed. Contact and more contact.

Bryn and Thea were integrated into the operative part of the program at this time. Increase the diversity of contact for Raun. Involve the girls for their brother's sake and for their own. Make sure they were not feeling alienated or deprived. Try to make them as much a part of Raun's journey as we were. More than just for selected moments, their ongoing involvement could be important and crucial. An entire family pulling together, whose common love and endeavor might really make the difference.

They were each given separate times to be with him. First they spent several days watching Suzi with Raun. We wanted to continue her momentum. Their contact was unstructured. They were told to be with him, love him, approve of him and reinforce any social contact he made. If they wanted, they could touch him, but if he pushed away they were to leave him alone. If he spun or rocked, they were told not to try to stop him . . . rather to imitate him until he went on to another activity.

Both Bryn and Thea were excited and willing. We impressed

upon them that if either of them wanted to stop working with Raun for a period of time or completely, it was certainly all right with us. Their participation was to be based purely on their wanting. We encouraged them to stay in touch with us, with themselves . . . their feelings and wants.

They were immediately swept into the adventure. Each work period was punctuated with their joys of relaying Raun's every reaction and accomplishment. They seemed to be natural teachers in their own right with their own sensibilities and deep sources of loving.

Five

What was merely a simple interaction for the normal one-and-a-half-year-old child was a confounding and complex experience for Raun. Trying to imitate us seemed to require intense effort and concentration on his part; though he was very quick at what he initiated or what he designed in behavior or activities, it was new gestures that originated from outside of him that he had extreme difficulty digesting.

The concept of imitiation of him grew. It became more than just a backdrop and sequence of our sessions. It became a central theme in our home. We knew that we were showing him that, with minimal effort, he could effect change and control. When he shook his head, we all did. When he smiled, everyone smiled. If he stuck out his tongue, everyone stuck their tongues out. Each time, he watched us with fascination and delight. Sometimes smiling. He would quietly regard our behavior. He was becoming more and more aware that he could set the pace.

Once he was confident that he was really in control, "Simon Says" was the order of the day. As we followed him into his movement, he would continually change . . . and then change again. Many dinners would lie cold as Suzi, I, Bryn, Thea and others would bang, click, kick and tap as Raun did. Enjoying ourselves. Loving this time that we had together, as Raun Kahlil was slowly coming to be with us.

His bathroom sessions were enriched with many new items: other types of insertion toys, more puzzles, brightly-colored plastic blocks, cups, picture books, and miniature musical instruments such as flutes, drums, tambourines, chimes and so on. Clay and finger paints were introduced. Play-Doh. Additional movement and touching games were designed. Swaying and humming to music.

Although his expertise was very limited and each step had to be precisely directed, we tried simplifying tasks and shaping his responses. If he just approximated a movement or partially completed an exercise, his attempts (when they occurred) were elaborately rewarded with soft cookies and physical affection. The specific accomplishments were less important than our intervention to help him want to learn and participate.

We used these toys and games as tools. Often, what appeared to be a simple deed had to be further broken down into extremely digestible components. For Raun to understand and master inserting a puzzle piece into its appropriate space, we would have to simplify it into three or four distinct steps. First, we would teach him how to pick up the piece. Then came learning the act of moving a piece with his hand from the place where he found it to the puzzle board. Next, the process of locating the correct form which matched the piece, and lastly, instructing him in the activity of turning and manipulating the piece until it fit into its spot. After he mastered each operation separately, they were slowly combined to form one entire sequence.

Our sensitivity to making the environment digestible for Raun was one of the basic fundamentals of our educational project. Each and every task was intently considered and redesigned to make it comprehensible.

During the fifth week of our program, Raun underwent another developmental check-up and examination. The diagnosis was still very much the same. We received no new input or information. There was encouragement for us in our attempts to move our son, yet strong words of skepticism. They wanted to caution us about unrealistic hopes.

A dance in the hallowed halls of medicine. Since future was

not our question, advice and concerns seemed obscure. Yet we did profit from the visit. Through their testing and plotting of Raun's abilities, we were able to compare these results with those of former work-ups. And we could see real progress not in terms of achievement but in comparison to the very beginning.

Our entire summer had become consumed by our endeavor to be with Raun, to reach him and say hello. Although we hired a woman to help with the housework, the pace was exhausting. For me, the hours in my office were mixed with continued research and reading. For Suzi, her days were swallowed up by our gigantic but beautiful new project—our son. Often, we were asked how we felt about being deprived of other activities and interests. The word "sacrifice" was even suggested. If a painter or sculptor begins a piece and works year after year on it, no one would ask him how deprived he feels. There would be the assumption that he expended all the energy and effort because he wanted to, because he enjoyed it. In our world, Raun was our piece of sculpture, as yet undated and incomplete. We do what we do because we want to and delight in our doing every day.

The modifications made in our life style did not preclude us from maintaining friendships we valued and some endeavors we enjoyed. Suzi did give up her sculpture for a time, but still continued with her music. Since I only slept five hours each night, I still had many hours available in addition to my time spent in the office or evolving a program for Raun. Teaching Option, writing, spending time with the girls were certainly important components of my life. In the evening, Suzi and I would usually find time for Yoga.

Our nightly rap sessions on Raun's progress and his changes continued. Each day we charted the program . . . each evening we evaluated his responsiveness. We devoted time to reviewing the attitudes of Bryn and Thea. We decided that although we were sensitive to the girls—their needs and their moods—we wanted more for them.

I set aside two afternoons each week to be with them. One at a time. Thea and I spent late afternoons at the duck pond, then had pizza and played pinball. Bryn and I went ice skating, then ate clams at McGuiness's. Loving them each individually, spending hours talking with them and discussing their feelings were important. We solicited their advice about Raun and the program, indicating to them how very important they were to us. Thea, who looked so much like Raun, would end our days together skipping up the driveway with me. Bryn, whose child-like womanhood was blossoming, asked to spend the last minutes of our afternoons together on the bed . . . hugging each other in silence.

With superhuman effort, Suzi worked tirelessly each day while finding the time and energy to spend loving hours in the evenings with the girls. My afternoons with them only accounted for a small portion of their time. The savior that summer was day camp, in which both Bryn and Thea were enrolled, actively and happily involved during the week. It was this diversion of camp that lessened their consciousness of just how much time and energy were devoted to Raun, although they were totally aware of his entire curriculum.

Concerned friends also assisted us by taking the girls from place to place on weekends while we were busy with Raun. Others participated in working with him for short interludes so Suzi could rest or go for an occasional bike ride.

There was Rhoda, intent on nursing her eternal diet, whose entry into the kitchen came with staccato comments and instructions for everyone . . . but whose soft and gentle concern touched us with her help with Thea, and at times, Bryn. She made a special effort to assist Suzi by transporting Bryn to friends' houses and by having her daughter spend hours playing with Thea.

Jerry J. was an eighteen-year-old version of the last Neanderthal man. His elephant imitations and soulfulness pervaded our home with a special quality of warmth, laughter, and caring. Often, he was a loving companion to the girls and performed lifeguard duties as they swam in the pool together. And vocal Laura, whose beautiful egocentric patterns of enthusiasm and poetry filled our rooms with light and excitement. Her mellowness, her old soul softened many summer days. Jointly, Jerry with his vibraphone and Laura with her soprano saxophone would play from the hilltop and fill our land with notes of jazz and melodies of themselves. Even Raun was alert to their music and its heartbeat.

And there was Nancy, whose shyness no longer resulted in her hands assaulting and hiding her face. She had first come to us at the age of thirteen as a mother's helper. Since she had been living with us on and off for the past five years, we considered her part of our family. Suzi and I were like surrogate parents, while the girls adopted her as their sister. She was with us now with her sensitivity and giving. Her baggy pants and boatlike shoes hid the blossoming of her body and camouflaged her womanhood . . . yet Nancy allowed herself the freedom to be herself with us and share her specialness. Her influence and help during these months contributed to the stability of our home and family.

The visits from gentle Jeffrey, our Yoga-styled string-bean partner in meditation, were always welcomed. He transformed his transcendental Eastern attitude and vegetarian cleanliness into graphics painted on the ceiling of our bedroom. Those silent, warm twilight evenings doing Yoga together as the haunting cello of Casals filtered through the outdoor speakers. Suzi, Jeffrey, Bryn, Thea and I assuming the Cobra position as we paid tribute to our bodies and our spirit.

Summer passing. Visits from brother Steve, a steady, yet radicalized edition of a free-thinking suburbanite, directing a drug-training program at a university hospital while negotiating daily contracts with his liberated wife. One afternoon, his hairy body parted the waters in our swimming pool as he dove in pursuit of Raun, who had just fallen in to take his first unauthorized swim.

And Laurie, Steve's wife, whose love and beliefs made it difficult for her to accept Raun's autism. She hoped for some magical solution that would restore him to being a communicative and playful little boy like her son, who was the same age.

There was also father Abe, whose athletic form projected the image of a man thirty years younger and whose studied mustache brought back nostalgic visions of William Powell's debonair portrayal of *The Thin Man.* He and his wife, Roz, stayed one week at our home, supplying slices of the past as they melted into the energized framework of our lives. A time for me to renew a love and affection for my father which had flowered in the nine years since the death of my mother. All this, while Roz played lovingly and easily with our children.

65

Evenings with Marv (or Merv, as Bryn called him affection-
ately) and Elise, a very special woman, our resident astrology
whiz currently eating her way through her third or fourth life
and loving it. Marv, whose handlebar mustache distinguished
his face and covered a multitude of sins. A fellow Option associate, whose knowledge and understanding became more pronounced and fascinating from day to day, whose comedy included routines from Gunga Din and the old Howdy-Doody
shows, whose warmth and concern were quiet and uncondi-
tional . . . and with us all the time.

Evenings of dialogue with Marshall and Joy. Like Chaplin
playing an existential ping-pong game with a hypothetical ball,
Marsh would mix the metaphor of his mathematics with eternity while Joy treaded water doing psychoanalytical therapy
before diving into the soup. Both with their razor-sharp intel-
lects entering into end games with me about the Option
Method and the Attitude.

Occasional horseback riding with Bryn or alone. Swimming
each morning and evening, throwing off the accumulated but
unspent energy of the day. All in all, an involved and exciting
summer. A summer in which Suzi had laid down her sculpture
chisel to pick up a tambourine for Raun.

Eight weeks of the program had elapsed. Beautiful. Difficult.
Frustrating. Rewarding. The progress had been just fantastic.
For another child, Raun's accomplishments might merely be
the new lesson learned in a day. But Raun's struggle and risk
taking to be with us and to explore the world were profoundly
heroic. The little boy who had looked through people now
sometimes looked at them, and even sometimes smiled at them.
The deaf one was now occasionally attentive to someone calling
him. The recluse was now genuinely participating and active.
Our "special" child was having more fun with himself and with
us. He was finding new ways to piece the world together and
make sense out of his perceptions.

*   *   *

One morning, Raun was with Suzi in the kitchen. He walked
over to the refrigerator and started to cry. Suzi asked him if he
wanted juice. He started to cry even more; Suzi knew that he

was at least trying to express himself. Rather than try to teach him a more socially acceptable procedure, she responded quickly by jumping up and immediately fulfilling his request by giving him the juice. We felt any form of communication with him was sensational. So as not to confuse him, we would allow him this route until he firmly understood that, by making a certain effort to communicate, he could trigger certain responses. Later that same day, he went over to the door and began to cry. Once Suzi opened it, he stopped his outcry and exited. An hour later, he stood at the bottom of the stairs and repeated his act.

He had moved into an active stage of communication. He wanted things external to himself and was now actively trying to get them. A breakthrough. He was bringing himself into our arena, becoming a participant in our family unit.

This week also marked the beginning of his mimicking words, when our cues and emphasis on language had their first results. Raun started to repeat words that were said to him, but always in the same tone, pitch and accent. He mouthed them into existence. But were they digested and assimilated into his system? The words had no meaning. He was echolalic, like many autistic children, parroting words exactly as he heard them without using them meaningfully as language. Yet, even though we knew he was still not communicating verbally, this was indeed an initial step. Perhaps this was his technique for holding what he heard before his mind's eye in order to extract its meaning, not unlike the student who repeats the teacher's question in order to hear it again and absorb it. We believed that if further development was possible it would not depend on rote training, but on the increased intensity of his wanting and increased awareness that others could be useful to him in attaining his goals.

Raun had made some dramatic leaps. He was a sky diver pulling the cord for the first time . . . a skier suspended in the air during his first downhill race.

*   *   *

We had been keeping notes from the inception of our program, but now we decided, at the end of the eighth week, to begin a formal journal, making entries in a log. The first part of this entry included a summary of Raun's behavior at the outset of our program.

LOG: EIGHTH WEEK—RAUN KAHLIL, 19 MONTHS—SCHEDULE 75 HOURS PER WEEK

Notes:

Raun two months ago: no social contact or interaction, no eye contact, enjoyed objects more than people, no language or gestures, no anticipatory gestures when being picked up; when he is held, he is limp and he only smiles to himself. Always self-stimulating—spinning, rocking, looking at hands, making repetitious motions with his fingers against his lips. Repeats strange movements with his hands. Pushes away from physical contact. Never cries to get out of his crib or to eat. Often appears deaf and blind. Stares constantly. Shows great desire for sameness. Throws everything and does not play.

Current: changes up to and including this week

—much less rocking movement; mostly rocks in his crib
—real eye contact established when playing certain games
—more facial expression
—still ignores people, but is somewhat more receptive to familiar people
—attentive to being called although most often will not come on request
—making less motion with his fingers against his lips
—hardly ever pushes away his mother
—has started to indicate wants by crying—first time definite communications effort
—starting to mimic words
—reacts to some spoken words when being addressed—car, cup, bottle, come, up, water
—for the first time, expressed anger in game environment—

when we tried to remove something he did not want to
give up
—for the first time, he did make an anticipatory arm gesture
when he was about to be picked up
—has begun to drink out of a glass when someone holds it
—cried twice when person he was playing with left the room
—occasionally follows people
—has started to feed himself with his fingers

No changes:
—still prefers the world of objects most of the time
—still spins—but will now give you the object to spin with
him
—still pushes away from people and physical contact
—generally, still throwing things
—still no gesture or verbal language development for general
communications (although using crying for the first time as
a form of communications)
—does not cry to get out of the crib or cry to indicate desire
to eat

General observations:
—has difficulty chewing and chokes on solid foods
—special desire for liquids . . . much more than solid foods.
Seems to be rejuvenated after drinking as if it were a stimulant, including water, juices, milk
—puts absolutely everything in his mouth
—reacts to repetitious saying of words or seeing the same
objects as if he had never heard or seen them before . . .
as if he does not retain them in his memory

*   *   *

It was a beautiful thrust. We were making a difference with
our intervention, although at the moment it was limited.

I began to notice Suzi seemed to be growing more and more
tired with the passing weeks. Her long blond hair was limp from

neglect. The soft creases in her forehead were deeper and more prominent. She was exhausted, yet her eyes still glistened and the spark was still with her. Wanting to be with her son, she was pushing at the perimeter of her resources, squeezing out all the juices each day.

I knew that for her this was a pilgrimage, not a burden or hardship. But I also knew that the time and energy level required had to be so high and intense so much of the time that her body was beginning to register the wear.

I approached Suzi with a new plan. Let us get volunteers or hire some other people to help. At first, Suzi thought that I might be doubting her or the quality of her input or its effectiveness. I assured her that was not the case, that I felt all of Raun's fantastic progress was due primarily to her and her efforts. But what about the abilities or the attitudes of others? Could we find people who would be able to participate in a way consistent with our approach and beliefs? I thought it was possible. We could teach them, train them and show them the Option approach. Finally, she smiled. It would be a welcomed addition.

Nancy, who was seventeen years old, was a natural as our first teacher-therapist. She had listened and learned Option over the past years. Her involvement with us and our family was intimate and binding. And her relationship to our crew was special; she loved the children as if they were her own. She said "yes" . . . she wanted to and was excited about being involved.

We also hired another girl, Maire. Different from Nancy, but sensitive and enthusiastic. She was a high school senior with an abiding interest in children. Ultimately, we spent more time working with her on attitude than showing her the tools and techniques of dealing with Raun. Initially, she was not confident. She was concerned we would judge her by Raun's progress. We assured her this was not our intention. He was always allowed his interests, his contacts and his rejections. She would come to understand that where he was or how he was feeling had nothing specifically to do with her . . . that he was choosing. She could only present things, suggest activities and involvements and try to facilitate his participation. Flowing with him would be crucial. Developing an environment in which he could freely want and, perhaps, get. She understood. She continued to learn and grow. And soon Maire too became a critical part and valued member of our growing "family" group.

We reduced Suzi's involvement to a still-incredible forty-five hours per week. Together, Nancy and Maire participated and worked between twenty and twenty-five hours a week. I became very impressed with the talents and capabilities of these very young nonprofessionals, who had more meaningful contributions and concern than most of the professionals that we had contacted. They were unindoctrinated . . . open and alive.

The motivational program continued and now the teaching of specifics became more preplanned. After initiating and instructing our new "teachers," Suzi caught up on some rest and spent extra hours with our daughters. She began to sculpt again.

Both of us monitored Raun's progress, watching carefully and helping him accept these new people in his life . . . introduction similar to the manner in which Suzi had reintroduced herself to her son eight weeks ago. Slowly. Nonaggressively. In our nightly rap sessions on attitudes during and after dinner, we spent hours discussing his echolalia. We wanted everyone to be supersensitive to all communications and yet also reward his mimicking, even though it had not as yet acquired any meaning. His words were flat and often spoken to the walls, his eyes vacant as his mouth created the sounds.

Six

On the highway heading home, the sun, baked crimson, lingered just above the road in my rear-view mirror. Humming across the pavement in my brown solar shuttle thinking about my son. Knowing that Raun was breaking through the walls, putting more of it together and coming toward us. His behavior and inabilities to absorb and digest . . . the enigma of some organic deprivation as yet undefined, some disconnected or disassembled circuitry. The system which catalogs and retrieves information from the memory cells of the cerebral cortex seemed inoperative. And, if so, how could we redo or alter what was already awry? It was simple . . . *we* couldn't. But maybe Raun could.

I was familiar with research that dealt with people who had suffered strokes and the eventual possibilities of "permanent damage." In many cases, it could be shown that specific masses of brain tissue and cells had been irrevocably destroyed. Autopsies showed large areas permanently damaged by scarring. And yet, in the face of this damage, some patients found new ways to talk, new ways to move . . . made new connections which allowed them to regain control over areas once paralyzed. They did not regain the functions of the destroyed cells, but rather used portions of the brain not previously utilized. Expanding their celluloid potential and frontier.

And why could some stroke victims make these seemingly miraculous jumps while others remained crippled and handicapped? Most professionals attribute it to motivation and wanting . . . an essential ingredient in the successful outcome of most serious operations and treatments. We knew that if we could get Raun to want to participate with us he would then make the new connections, open new channels. He could do it or at least he would try, not by simple training or rote memory, not by conditioning, but by the energy and internal efforts that would come as the fruits of his own desire.

*　　*　　*

That evening, before we put Raun to bed, we sat with him in our bedroom and watched him walk around and play with our shoes. Suddenly, he became captivated by an image he saw while passing in front of the mirror. Although he had certainly passed by the mirror many times, tonight for him there was something notably different. He stopped and was immediately mesmerized by a commanding form—his own.

He surveyed himself. He moved back and forth from left to right. He walked directly to the mirror and touched nose to nose with his reflection. His eyes were like electric lights. He moved out of the path of the mirror and then slowly looked back into it. As he did, he met his face. He moved directly forward again . . . touched his stomach, then his head. He began to shout some wild noise . . . a cry of incredible excitement and joy. He began to grunt and laugh with elation. Raun Kahlil had discovered himself. I turned to Suzi amazed and dazzled. Tears were streaming down her face. I could feel the wetness under my eyes as I realized that I too was crying. The first day of creation . . . a new dimension. He had found himself and it was a joyful experience.

Through the tears we continued to observe our son. He played with himself in a way that he had never played with anyone or anything before. He was positively animated and engaged. Talking some mumbled and primitive language, making grunts to his reflection while playing hide-and-seek with himself.

Carefully, he explored his hands, then his feet, then his hair. He touched and watched himself simultaneously. He would pick up his pajama top to expose his belly to his new partner. For twenty beautiful and gripping minutes, Raun said hello to himself. And this was a meeting that he was now ready for . . . that he had wanted and had enjoyed. The oasis in the desert was himself.

Suzi and I spent a quiet and dreamy evening. We walked by the surf at a beach we had driven to. No need to talk. We held each other as we strolled. The water rocked back and forth in its moontides. The glimmers of light bounced between us as we moved through the thick mist. Ebbtide.

*   *   *

Someone is still with Raun every minute of every day, providing contact and the bombardment of stimulation. The crew, all of us, are working with him more excited by our sensing the unfolding of a newly-developed chapter. After his finding himself in the mirror, he became more purposeful about his activity and involvement. More premeditated. Perhaps now he was equipped with new understanding: the awareness of his presence and his physical body, its visual components and complexity, its fleshiness and beauty.

The following is an account of Raun's typical day. When possible, this schedule was followed seven days a week.

DAILY SCHEDULE

8:30   Raun probably has been up a half hour in his crib with his toys, which he usually has by this time thrown out of his crib. He is now taken out, dressed and goes downstairs by himself (backwards slide). His breakfast is with Suzi, sometimes at the table, sometimes in the bathroom. Much verbalizing and audio stimulus.

74

9:15 Generally, he and Suzi go into bathroom with his work material and music. Games based on personal and continual interpersonal relations, with food as rewards and reinforcement (each cooperative situation is immediately followed by a piece of food or cookie). Games include: insertion box with at least thirty different shapes, four or five wood insertion puzzle games with hand knobs (with Suzi making sounds for all animals and much articulating of nouns), truck with seven connecting pieces, tool game toy, music instruments to bang and blow, insertion and building cups, clay and Play-Doh, crayons and chalk, mounted pictures of family members and other objects to be shown for possible identification. Music exercises included moving arms, feet and torso with Suzi to the tempo of music and at random. Body-parts-identification games for the purpose of developing gestures (pointing) and language stimulation with naming of parts and activities. Touching interludes. Attempts to use books, look at pictures, turn pages . . . also to utilize the touch and small materials.

10:30 Break from confined work area—go for a walk, play peekaboo, try some other toys, give him some food . . . constant interaction.

11:00 Back into the bathroom for more structured working and games.

12:00 Finish morning stimulation sessions—another walk, or a car ride, a trip to the park, to the store, a visit with other children.

1:00 Nap.

2:30 Awake and down for lunch.

3:00 Short work session in the bathroom.

3:30 End of bathroom session—playing in the park, a bike ride . . . also time for Bryn and Thea to function as playmate/therapists.

4:00 Special helper (Maire or Nancy) arrives and takes Raun to the park, onto the swings, with physical games and much verbal stimulus.

4:30 Bathroom work session with helper.

5:30	Finishes . . . time now spent with other members of the family or teaching group, jumping on the bed, random play, more games, more physical stimulation.
6:30	Dinner with entire family and student teacher or teachers.
7:00	Additional work session in the family den.
8:00	Work session ends.
8:30	Raun to sleep.

*   *   *

One of the other difficulties that Raun was having was his inability to eat solid foods. At each meal, we would attempt to teach him to chew as we tried to convert his baby-food diet into a more rounded meal. One night, he grabbed a handful of french-fried potatoes from a bowl and shoved them into his mouth. A comic image with swollen cheeks and the amused look of a clown. Before we had a chance to dislodge the excess food from his bulging mouth, he swallowed part of it. Quickly, he was in trouble.

It became apparent that the food was stuck in the passageway. He began to struggle desperately with himself, pushing his fingers into his neck to help himself. His eyes opened wide, pushing outward from his head as if to grab air through his vision. We picked up his arms and slapped his back. It was not working. Christ!

Now he was having tremendous difficulty breathing. I picked him out of the chair, opened his mouth and searched for the food with my fingers. No use. I turned him upside down and began shaking him. Raun was struggling more now. His body jerked spasmodically in response. I put him upside down again, slapped his back, hit his buttocks. Impossible. An every-evening occurrence had quickly assumed the proportions of an unthinkable nightmare. Everyone was out of their seats. I could see all the rush of movement in my peripheral vision as I searched myself desperately for something else to do. Shock the digestive track . . . send a ripple through the system that would make him vomit. Suzi held him upside down. I found the soft part of the abdomen just below his rib cage with one hand and slammed the palm of my other hand upward into his body. His entire body answered with a harsh grunt and immediately the potatoes and contents in his stomach came tumbling to the floor.

My hands began to shake as I looked at Suzi's numbed expression. She held him to her. Raun coughed, but seemed to recover quickly. He looked at us with great relief. His eyes glittered as he gave us a glance that seemed to say "thanks."

Short panting breaths dominated my body as my ribs strained under the constant and rapid pounding. Suzi and I again mirrored each other through the tension in our eyes. She was chalk white, but with great effort managed to squeeze out a smile. I began to laugh. Raun was here!

We decided that moment to immediately implement a crash effort to teach Raun how to consume solid foods. We would first establish eye contact, then have him watch us insert food into our mouths, chew it with great exaggeration and then swallow it. We repeated this over and over. Finally, Suzi would place a soft but solid food into his mouth. Usually he just let it sit there on his tongue or let it fall out. Suzi then would talk to him as she worked his bottom set of teeth with her hands . . . closing and opening them against his upper set. Each meal, we repeated this exercise. Then, every so often, she felt the participation of the muscles of his jaws. It took almost two weeks until we started to note real progress.

*　　*　　*

Saturday and Sunday were merged together as we relaxed into our individualized life-style. Many weekend afternoons were often reserved for our miniature indoor bon fires. Bryn, Thea and I would gather up the stubby logs piled at the side of our house. Thea always warned me not to give her heavy ones. Bryn inevitably asked for more and more logs until the strain on her arms became apparent in her face. The three of us stacked the wood in and out of the living-room fireplace.

Packing the paper in very special places, we made a base for the flames to begin. Suzi checked to see if the air conditioning was still on . . . our late-summer antics required immediate cooling. And then, as we all sat around, I lit the twisted paper and ignited the many corners of our creation

. . . always careful to have Raun break from his sessions at those moments in order to be with us . . . to watch with fascination the dancing and dazzling flames. Reds, purples and white. As the fire began to roar, Bryn and Thea would cheer and clap. The stereo would belt out some Bach played by the Modern Jazz Quartet.

Once we were sure of the success of our fire, we would all clear the center of the floor of furniture, leaving the room barren before the hearth. Bryn would bring in some bean bags while Thea grabbed the pillows from the bedroom. In two minutes, using the soft cushions for support, we intertwined with each other in varied positions on the floor to enjoy the fire and each other. Bryn's head leaning on my legs as Thea's feet draped over my stomach. Suzi diagonally across my chest. The Big Bear had become the big bear rug.

Within a half hour, we were joined by Jerry and Laura, who extended our new creature—our evolving family. Then Nancy arrived. Anticipating the ringing telephones, we disconnected them for the remainder of the day. Raun kept playing and poking at the fire. Jerry began tossing a ball to Bryn, who returned it through her giggles. Thea asked Laura to play pick-up sticks. Suzi kissed me and whispered that she was very happy. Our family expanded again with the arrival of Steve and Laurie with their two sons, Jordy and Ari. They melted into various parts of the room, the fire still maintaining central dominance. It set the tone and mood, which was essentially peaceful and melodic.

These were beautiful times, when talking and doing became secondary to our being with and flowing with the people we loved. A time when the good feelings of each of us touched everyone in the room. An hour set aside while I did Option with Laura, helping her investigate the beliefs underlying the discomfort she was experiencing. Suzi and Raun were experimenting on Jerry's vibraphone. Bryn and Thea swayed to the rhythm. Nancy stared into the flames. The voices and the music blended into a symphony. Mellow. A togetherness we all treasured. Poignantly aware of being well loved.

*   *   *

As the program continued, we were more aware of Raun's growing desire to make different facial expressions and communicate. Playing in the mirror with himself had become one of his favorite games. He was increasingly conscious of being capable of affecting his environment. Manipulating us by taking our hands, pulling us toward objects he wanted and then crying. The message was loud and clear. I want. I want.

It was beautiful. In the morning he took Suzi's hand and led her to the refrigerator to show her that he wanted juice. In the evening of that same day, he pulled me to the bottom of the staircase to illustrate to me that he wanted to go upstairs. The second-floor area for Raun was his private world, where he often wanted to go to be alone. We always allowed him this, although we would intercede after extended periods of time.

When we put a glass of water on the table, he would go after it once he had seen it. We would help him hold it in his tiny hands. Prior to this day, he was only motivated to eat or deal with liquids that were put directly in front of him. Now he knew. Now he extended himself. He was a programmer, finally mastering a more effective use of his computer . . . comprehending the sorting and processing of data.

We had also noted his becoming increasingly attentive to people. More involved. Almost caring. And the reasons were perhaps obvious . . . people were becoming increasingly useful and helpful to him in getting what he wanted. In the games and in physical contact, people were becoming a source of joy and loving. It was even compounded. When he would spin, he would solicit our interaction. Giving us the top of a jar or plate so that we could also have our turn. Game playing with us. This was so much more meaningful than the parallel imitation of several weeks ago.

There was now another hurdle to jump. Initially, Raun had used crying as a means of asking and articulating. We permitted it and reinforced it as a means because we believed that for him any form of communication was far more important than the specific method he chose. We also did not want to extinguish what had just begun by confusing him with different or even incomprehensible directions. But now Raun was much more aware of himself. His wants. His abilities. Strong enough in this mode, we thought, to be capable of accepting and dealing with change. It would be done slowly. Each time he cried, we would ask him what he wanted, give him what we believed to be the answer and then point to it. Over and over again. One hundred times each day.

Almost each week brought with it new accomplishments— new breakthroughs. Yet, I lingered on an area I knew to be critically important to his ability to think and ultimately talk.

Each evening, I put him through the same test that I had been doing for weeks, hoping one day to help him to be able to accomplish the near-impossible. I would greet him in the kitchen and show him a cookie. When he put his hand up for it I would slowly move it while talking to him and he would follow it with his eyes. Then I would carefully and obviously put the cookie behind a piece of paper. He would lose it as it disappeared from his immediate vision and stand there confused. He still could not hold it . . . keep it in his memory so that it was available as an image even though it was out of view. He still had limited connecting power and limited or no capability to solidify images in his mind for future referral. Perfecting and developing this area was critical for creating the landscape upon which he could build language.

This was our game. Raun's and mine. The rehearsal for perhaps another time.

LOG: NINTH WEEK—SAME SCHEDULE, THREE ACTIVE TEACHERS

Changes:
  —Eye contact becoming excellent
  —More attentive to familiar people now and even short durations of attention for new people
  —Absolutely no hand watching this week
  —More expression of wants by pulling and crying
  —Listens to requests: i.e., go here, take my hand, put it back, wait, come, go get it, eat, sit down
  —Now initiates game playing and social contact—he will give us objects for us to spin with him

80

—More active interest in game-related activities such as peekaboo, insertion toys, puzzles
—More possessive of objects; for the first time he will now actually fight for things and will cry if something he wants is removed
—Starting to hold glass by himself and drinking by himself . . . but this is very inconsistent
—Will follow people in and out of rooms, especially his workroom
—Has started to chew solid foods without incident
—Enjoys playing with himself in front of the mirror . . . goes up and down the glass with his hands, playing peekaboo with his image. Also looking at other people through the mirror
—Now starting to solicit some physical contact . . . seems to enjoy it at times
—Comes to his mother and teachers when strangers are around
—Starting to gesture: some pointing and banging at the things he wants
—Responds to more complex verbal suggestions: "Raun wants bottle," "Wait a minute," "Raun, stand still" (when putting on clothes).

No changes:
—Still prefers the inanimate world when he has the opportunities outside his work sessions
—Still very absorbed by spinning objects
—Still does not indicate or cry to get out of the bed in the morning or after naps
—Still does not use verbal language to communicate
—Throws everything he gets his hands on

Further observations:
—Aware that the quality of his responses is much better in places like the bathroom or even in the car where there are few distractions
—Imitating more sounds and physical acts (mouthing, cock-

ing of head, jumping, crawling, running, hitting the tambourine as instructed, blowing, etc.)
—More positive interaction when he initiates and controls
—Knows the sound of the car and doorbell . . . looks in the appropriate direction when he hears them
—Curls his fingers to one side of his face if he is agitated
—Has a specific way of turning away from people as he is smiling
—Gets notably upset when his sisters cry . . . tries to manipulate them to smile, approaching them, even touching them at times.

*   *   *

Raun came down with Suzi from his room one day not yet fully dressed. She put him on the floor for a few seconds in order to make coffee. Raun quickly grabbed his shoes and tried to put them on. He struggled with them. I sat beside him to help. Little by little, we were able to get his shoes on with him directing the process. As soon as we finished, he ripped both of them off and began again. I aided him again. Once they were on his feet, off they came. His tiny fingers worked busily. He was excited and animated with his new accomplishment. He must have repeated it over thirty times. Finally, he was exhausted.

In the afternoon, Suzi took time out to practice the saxophone, one of her new involvements, which had begun only a few weeks ago. Laura was her teacher. The notes came careening out of the sensually curved bellows of the horn . . . invading our home with the brassy dissonance of sounds too flat or too sharp. The crackling noise was a beginner's shrill chorus.

Every time Suzi began, Raun would actually run from the clamor . . . out of the room. Sometimes, he cried in protest at this assault. His stated opinion was loud and clear . . . made with visible lucidity and impact. In contrast, we, Bryn, Thea, I and loving friends, were more accepting of Suzi's starts. We had seen many of them. Her on-again off-again periods of playing the piano. Then her affair with the guitar and the writing of her own music and lyrics. All those free concerts with us as her captive audience. And now the saxophone. While Raun ran and hid, we rejoiced in the fact that at least it wasn't the tuba or trumpet that she had decided to fall in love with.

* * *

It was the beginning of our eleventh week in the program. As I came through the side door after a day working in tinsel town, I bumped right into Raun, who was standing by the table. He peered up at me very casually, brought his right hand up from his side as if to take the oath of office, and then pushed his fingers up and down against his palm. He was waving hello.

Dumbfounded, I waved back. He stayed with me for several seconds and then looked away. What a simple and profound hello . . . the best I ever had. Three months before if I had walked through the door and thrown a hand grenade Raun would have never so much as flinched or looked at me. Now this little man was greeting me. My number was coming in. We were both the winners.

There was still enough time for Raun and me to play our favorite nongame before Suzi put him to bed. I took a cookie off the counter and showed it to him. I put it in the center of the floor, calling his attention to it. And, as he watched, I ever so slowly placed a newspaper over it, hiding it from his view. He paused, staring at the paper for almost a minute. Then, with very little overt expression of interest, he walked over to the paper and sat beside it. He was studying the pictures on the face of the paper. His eyes moved slowly across the entire page and lingered on the edges. Suzi and I looked at each other, waiting silently. We had seen it before, each night, and nothing had changed.

But then, quite easily, Raun moved the paper with his hands, sliding it to his right until the cookie was uncovered. Carefully, he picked it up and ate it. A random accident? A quick cataloging of the event . . . seemingly without premeditation or purposefulness. But our analysis was from the outside looking in. Try again. Take the chance.

I took another cookie and showed it clearly to Raun. I put it on the floor in another part of the room and slowly placed another piece of newspaper over it. From the corner of my eyes, I noted his intensity, an animalistic quality, poised to strike. My neck tightened as a flutter of energy ran through the upper part of my torso. As soon as I stepped out of the way, he moved swiftly in my tracks, lifted the newspaper and quickly plunged the cookie into his mouth. Amazing. He seemed filled with a new sense of authority, a new confidence. Had it really happened? Does this mean he can hold images now in his memory and use them?

I grabbed a handful of cookies. I put one under the base of a light chair in his full view. He followed, quickly lifted the chair and took the cookie. I put another on the counter out of his view. He again followed, lifted his hand and felt around on the top of the counter. His little fingers walked across the formica until finding its mark. He grabbed the cookie and rewarded himself. A cookie on top of the chair. A cookie under the pillow of the couch. A cookie hidden in my clenched fist, which he soon assaulted and forced open. Determination. We were drenched in our own outrageous exuberance. And he was too.

He was enjoying this game immensely, excited to pursue and find the food. We played for over a half hour. Maybe I never really believed that he would be able to do it. It was awesome to get so much more than I had ever envisioned, to want it and allow it not to be, in your mind . . . to want it freely and have the gift of getting it. Like finding a diamond when you are looking for glass.

*　　*　　*

Next day while I was at the office, Suzi called on the phone, excited and supercharged.

"He really moved last night with the cookies, Barz. Before with the puzzle, you know, he could only deal with one piece at a time and only with explicit directions. But this morning, when I gave him the puzzle, mixed up all the pieces and scrambled everything, he worked it out. Completely. Without any help or guidance. It's like he can retain more, use more. Oh, wow! He's switched on like a thousand-watt bulb! I'm so excited for him . . . for me, for all of us."

She knew that she could show him games and toys that were going to have more impact beyond just motivating and socializing. If he could use what he remembered, he could now be capable of learning much more. The depths of his mind had an opening on the surface. Feeling so high. I said: "You did a great job, babes . . . really a super job."

Suzi didn't answer, but I could hear her sobbing softly on the other end of the line.

"I love you, Suz."

Another pause as she began to find her way back, grasping at her composure.

"Don't mind me, I'm really very, very happy and very silly. I'm just celebrating."

Suzi had seen the ramifications of his breakthrough . . . his new ability to remember. We both realized what it could mean, but kept ourselves in touch with not expecting it. Allow Raun to develop his own capabilities at his own rate. To know that when he wanted to and could, he would.

Although much of the time Raun was still remote and aloof, his being with us was becoming more productive, the interaction more meaningful. In the park, he would now actually go up to other children. On one occasion with Suzi, Raun looked directly at one little boy standing near the swings and smiled. Then, with no apparent warning, he hugged the child and put his face to the child's face. The other little boy quickly became frightened and began to cry. Raun immediately backed off. Confused and concerned. He mimicked his little friend—crunching up his face as if he too were sad. After several minutes, when the child's sobbing stopped, Raun moved cautiously toward him and softly stroked his arm. His new friend looked at Raun curiously. An act of communion and affection by a very delicate and oftentimes frail human being. An act that was unsolicited and self-motivated.

This day the sun began to rise in Raun's eyes.

*　　*　　*

There was no letting-up on the frenetic pace for us, or for Raun. Each event precipitated another. Each introduction brought new growth. Enter Victoria. Big Vic, who can act out more beauty nonverbally than a poet can with words, who can find creativity in every sound and movement, who can harness more energy than a perpetual-motion dream machine. A friend, loved and loving, she worked with handicapped and emotionally-disturbed children as a music and dance therapist. She wanted to try working with Raun. She was vivacious but gentle; aggressive but caring. Her blond hair capped an impressive presence, her blue eyes finding flight outside their sockets.

The first day, before Raun had really had the opportunity to know her, Vikki began with the pilgrimage into the bathroom. Immediately upon closing the door, Raun registered discomfort. Scared. Nervous. Skittish. So unlike him . . . a fracture in his usual passivity. He began to cry. And cry, until the momentum grew into hysteria. He was choking and sobbing at the same time.

Vikki tried to come close, to be with him and soothe him. He banged his response on the door. Out! He wanted out. She responded and opened it. Raun ejected himself through the doorway. He scrambled through the house, searching frantically. Finally, he found what he wanted . . . Suzi. Running to her, he pushed himself between her legs and pressed his tear-streaked face against her thighs. His little hands clutched at blue denim. His small form leaned on a tower of comfort. Suzi stroked his hair. He accepted her affection.

Just a standard recurring interaction between a mother and child? An unsung union that takes place many times each day in most families? Part of the loving, part of the mothering. And yet, for Suzi and for me, this was a very special and singular event. Raun, nineteen months old, had never solicited anyone's help for protection or for the soothing of his anxieties. It had never been a question for him. Indeed, it had never even seemed to matter who he was with at any given time. But now a binding union had become solidified. For the first time, he had ventured outside of himself to form a strong, trusting attachment to Suzi.

For her, a mother who had waited almost two years for her child to seek her, to want her warmth and loving, it was a deeply private and personal experience. Her son was coming home.

*　　*　　*

86

Vikki continued to try to work with Raun for almost a week. The first few minutes of each session, Suzi joined them until she knew that Raun was comfortable. Yet, after only three or four days, it became apparent that Vic was having difficulty. Her brand of stimulus bombardment seemed too hectic for him. Her finely-developed talents and tools were not working. Raun was not responsive . . . not participating.

Confused and concerned, Vikki's attitude began to change. She started to believe that something was wrong with her, that Raun's withdrawal was a statement about her ineffectiveness. In the sessions, she focused on her own questions, her own doubts.

Raun became more and more difficult. We had round-table discussions about the expanding problem. Vikki finally decided to wait until Raun was older and, perhaps, more receptive so that she could work her magic. She had had no previous experience with children so young. Wait a couple of months and then see. We all concurred.

In this experience, we saw the confirmation of the validity of one of our original premises. As long as we demanded measurable signs of Raun's learning as evidence of our own capabilities, we somehow displayed our pressure to him and did things that were counterproductive. It was a trap that could lead to pushing him and making the sessions conditional on a level of performance. A pressure, a "must," a "should," that Raun would push against. And did.

Bryn, at dinner, said she was becoming more and more excited with her brother and their developing relationship. She loved when he responded. She said that she believed that he cared now. Chattering enthusiastically about his ease with puzzles and games. A proud teacher . . . proud of herself and her pupil, sensitive to his wants and relaxed about his closing her out. Bryn was growing as much as Raun in their loving interchange. A beautifully attentive and compassionate young woman.

The depth of her insight was developing rapidly. She was also reading more. Even the exploration of her own talents had increased.

Inventiveness and grabbing the limelight were the most apparent by-products of her energy. She had taken violin lessons and now her practicing had given birth to nightly serenades at mealtime. Although we did not protest, the strings of her instrument seemed to cringe as they sounded their sour notes. Bryn was also an enthusiastic pianist, though she tended to pound and hammer the keyboard of the piano, which she was also studying. Her lessons in acting and dance were transformed into a platform for performances. She would do modern interpretive choreography for us on many occasions . . . always without an invitation. Often, she did expert imitations of family and friends to our delight and amusement. Bryn was blossoming . . . more than her years.

Thea talked less than Bryn about Raun's growth and more about her having fun with him. She had a lovely and incisive capacity to be with him on his level, to play as a peer, to engage him and create a carefree physical interaction. Her relationship was less verbal, more intuitive. Sometimes, out of her own enthusiasm, or perhaps jealousy, Thea would push him to respond. Either Suzi or I would gently intercede and show her alternative ways to play with him. From beneath the bangs and deep-set eyes would come an impish gaze. Hedging, but wanting to know more. She was so visceral in her relationships.

And Thea still spent long hours by herself drawing and painting . . . creating fantasy images of her family, her friends and her daydreams. Loving and expressionistic. Often, she would draw beautiful and detailed pictures and present them to us as gifts. Statements of her affection. Descriptions of her feelings. Her figures were captured in movement and flight, animated and colorful. Blue hair. Red faces. Yellow noses. Even her small clay people were messages modeled in a language she loved and treasured.

*   *   *

Raun sat on the back seat of my bicycle for an early-morning ride. We pedaled through the neighborhood, accompanied by Bryn. Raun sitting quietly, staring at the trees and houses as they flew by. He was hypnotically captivated by the motion. Movements that helped him slide into that peaceful and meditative state. We arrived at the park . . . the very same one where the word "autism" had sprung to life in my head.

These past two and a half months seemed centuries away from that time. Yet, as I put my son on the swing and looked intently into his eyes, I realized that, although his progress had been dramatic and sometimes spectacular, daring and deliberate, Raun still remained far below the normal operating capacity of other children his age. In language and sociability, this nineteen-month-old boy continued to function at an eight- or nine-month level. Only his large motor skills and some small motor activities were appropriate to his chronological age. His motor skills and reflexes were far outpacing all other areas of development.

Reviewing. I recounted the achievements to keep myself in touch and set off the balloons of his parade.

Beginning from the grip of his own inertia, Raun had moved down the human river and allowed himself to float into the mainstream. He was learning even to jump the rapids, learning to use the currents. To make the world his. To be with others. To permit contact. To express some of his wants. He was learning how to use his memory and retain objects in his mind. All of which was awesome . . . all of which would serve as foundations for further expansion and growth. At the very least, it gave him additional tools and know-how to deal with himself and his environment.

If he moved no further, I would feel rewarded in our work, knowing that in touching our son we had touched what was most beautiful in ourselves. This he had given us, by being there . . . by being Raun.

*　　　*　　　*

Midnight. The telephone ringing. Voices pierced through years of silence. Friends from California, coming through New York in less than two days and wanting to be with us. To pull up the curtain of time and renew a long and oftentimes intense relationship. We welcomed it.

Two days later. The air was humid as the heat of the day lingered. A huge, sleek, twenty-eight-foot motor home rolled into our driveway. The sound of its horn was like the baritone

89

growl of an old Santa Fe diesel whipping across an opened railroad crossing. Bryn and Thea came charging out the front door. Suzi and I followed. The huge mechanical beast was huffing and puffing even though the ignition had been turned off. My friend Jesse appeared in its doorway . . . mellow and tired as our arms interlocked. Our usual robust Russian embrace was now softened by the mood. His wife, Suzi, jumped from the truck into Suzi's arms. Then we all embraced. My face showered with the warmth and moisture of kisses. The distance and time that separated us disappeared for these frozen moments. Then Suzi, my Suzi, turned to the parked dinosaur, grabbing their children into her arms and hugging her first hello. Strange to be meeting them now for the very first time. Julie . . . sensitive, with her piercing eyes, and very womanly at seven years old. Cheyenne, only four, but already a stage-stealing comic with his red curly hair and baggy pants. And their little people met our little people, dancing their hellos and skipping their excitement into the house.

We stood with Jesse and Suzi under the clear sky, smiling at each other, touching through our eyes. Feeling the old closeness yet still tasting the distance. Jesse seemed slightly removed behind a haze of hard work. Once the lead singer and writer for a rock group called The Youngbloods . . . now he was starting to tour with his own act . . . Jesse Colin Young. For him, this was like beginning again. Moving up in a new context. This weekend, he was slated to give three evening performances at the Nassau Coliseum.

The four of us talked and reviewed our lives, exchanging the highlights and most dramatic experiences of recent years. We looked at their faces and saw in slow motion the images footnoting fourteen years of friendship. Remembering Jesse and me sitting on a bathroom floor in a dormitory at Ohio State in the middle of the night, writing songs, drinking watered-down beer and singing in harmony as the Midwest slept. He with his guitar and me with my writing pad. A time for birth . . . seventeen years old and still just touching the surface of who we were. Yet, in the brotherhood of those years, we were so very close. Inseparable. We enjoyed a relationship grounded beneath the quicksand of our changing moods. We were one together. A camaraderie that I have never quite experienced again.

Raun Kahlil: Lost in his own world, his eyes glaze over as he drifts away, staring hypnotically into space.

Fascination with inanimate objects: In a world devoid of human contact, Raun fixes intensely on a small cup. At times he would investigate a single object for hours at a time.

At twenty-three months, Raun can absorb and maintain contact in a way impossible six months ago. Here he is photographed by his father during one of his highly structured work/play sessions with his mother.

Praise and affection (left): Raun completes puzzle in bathroom classes and receives animated support from his mother.

Body identification and language training (below): Suzi helps Raun identify and say "mouth."

Shape differentiation (right): with the accent on increasing small motor activity skills, Raun explores board with knobs and doors.

Inserting shapes (below): Raun develops hand–eye coordination and learns colors with the guidance of Suzi.

Accent on physical contact and affection: Suzi uses touching and kisses as natural expressions of human contact and love in all play and teaching sessions.

Language and letter identification: Raun is introduced to letters by his father. Exploring the basic components of words through sound and touch becomes a structured function in expanding the concept and use of language.

Strong family unit contact: Barry, Suzi, sisters Bryn and Thea join in one of the many family group work sessions in which all participate in the exploration of books and pictures as an aspect of human contact and learning.

Responding to cues (top right): Raun interacts with his parents during lessons for the development of hand–eye coordination, figure–ground differentiation, identification of colors and shapes.

Maintaining contact through imitation (bottom right): Suzi and sisters Bryn and Thea rock with Raun to show approval and love when he withdraws and rocks alone. Imitation and participation are essentials of the program.

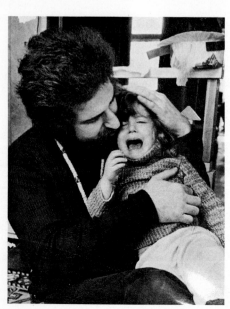

Physical expressions of human affection: After several months into the program, when Raun permitted, loving and consoling were always expressed with body contact to increase sensitivity and comfort with physical interaction.

Jesse recalled our motorcycle escapades in Pennsylvania while I was still going to college. Disappearing for weekends with Suzi on top of my beautiful and dignified BMW. Riding side by side along the Delaware River, sucking in the warm smells of the moist air. Cruising through the endless rows of cornfields. Sitting together in the meadows with wine, cheese and bread as we shared the summer sun. Years later, we drank espresso in Café Figaro, where Kerouac and Ginsberg had been only a decade before.

We had shared evenings and weekends many years ago as I too extended my reach for a cloud: writing stories, plays and poetry. A mound of rejection slips decorated my desk as Suzi played breadwinner. The completion of the first novel, which became a last hurrah. Abandonment of writing. My turning toward the commercial world of motion pictures and advertising. Being propelled by a ferocious drive. Jesse's direction was irrevocable. Mine . . . always tentative. Still exploring.

Now they would be with us for six days, easily integrated into our lives and our home. Mornings with Suzi working her normal schedule with Raun as Jesse's Suzi joined to help and experience our enigmatic son. The other children mixing like fast friends. The conversations ebbing and flowing as we sipped more wine; discussions about Option and teaching the Method.

Jesse and I reached for each other, searching to pick up the thread. For each of us, the years had taken a certain toll . . . and yet we each felt more enriched and happier than ever before. I spoke of my fantasy of a mountaintop in New Hampshire where I could give away land to each of my friends and start a special community. We played out our dreams together, talking them through.

Opening night. Endless lines of cars creeping into huge parking lots at the Coliseum as we sped swiftly through special back entrances accessible only to the performers. All eight of us packed into our car. Down the ramp under the building. Walking through long underground corridors until arriving at the dressing rooms. Beer and bourbon. Chatter and trivia. A tension in the room developing.

No seats available for us. We were to take the children and sit on stage with them. The theatre was in the round. A hush blanketed the audience as Bill Graham jumped on the stage.

Memories of Fillmore East. He made his announcement and introduced Jesse. Wild applause assaulted the stage from every direction. A deafening roar as the energy focused and bounced toward the entertainers, infecting them.

And then it began. The music ripped through the speakers, almost throwing us off the stage. It would take me the entire concert to adjust. Suzi was mesmerized. Not just a concert, an experience.

We would come back the next evening and the next. Each time with Bryn and Thea, to share the texture of this floodlight world. Its beauty. Its special brand of community. All of it . . . unforgettable.

The Youngs stayed one final day after their last performance before going south with their tour. When they left, we were grateful to them. For the love. For the fanfare. For the momentary diversion from Raun's silence. For the new experiences which embraced our children. For the opportunities to rekindle good feelings with old friends and to explore the changing tides of our lives.

Seven

Our search for this little man, for his dignity and specialness not only brought our original family closer together, but created a new and larger family unit . . . including his new teachers and the many others who helped. It was as if, through Raun, there was a loving that was spreading, that was infecting all of us around him. Could this be part of his meaning? Could this be part of the gift that he was? Being with him, loving him was like sitting on the edge of the well of life . . . experiencing birth and rebirth, being washed continually by the ripples of being in touch and finding in another the very best of yourself.

My life was bursting with discoveries and such very warm feelings, extending the softness of myself. Suzi grew more determined, more powerful and more radiant each day. Bryn became increasingly more tolerant and accepting. Thea more animated and vocal. Nancy bubbled with our growing love. Maire, more comfortable and confident from week to week, was really hooked on the little boy with soft blond ringlets. And Raun. Yes, Raun was an evolving human being.

—Expresses more anger, especially when objects are taken from him

—He initiates contact to get some help . . . by taking someone's hand and leading that person to a door to get outside or into a room, to get to a table or on a chair

—Much playing of peekaboo . . . he initiates . . . he will pull you, he will even chase you as well as be chased by you

—Enjoys other children . . . laughs and cries when they do; attentive to them and imitates them

—Tries to get on the chair by himself at the dinner table

—Initiates dancing when he hears music

—Shows still more understanding of receptive language

—Now repeats what you say in less time between verbal stimulus and his response, but still echolalic

—Has become bored with some kinds of playing . . . rolling balls, stacking blocks

—Plays very well with puzzles, but always turns them on the reverse or blank side and also upside down. Always looks at the pieces this way, finally correcting the positioning when reinserting back into the form

—Drinks out of a glass and eats solid food without incident and on his own most of the time

—Uses things that we don't want him to touch (lamps, glasses, etc.) to tease us: i.e., he will not open glasses cabinet when alone, but will immediately do it when he knows we are in the room

—Seems to be genuinely excited when his mother, father, teacher or other family members enter the house

—Still pushing off from physical fondling . . . but will stay with it longer in interaction with his mother

—Holds brush in hand and will attempt to brush his hair on request.

No changes:
  —When he is not approached or is not being worked in sessions, he still chooses to be alone . . . still chooses objects over people
  —Still spinning, but not as much as previously
  —Still does not cry to get out of the crib or to get food
  —Still does not use verbal language to communicate
  —Throws things extensively, especially when left by himself even only for very short periods of time.

*   *   *

Raun was like music that had no words. Yet we knew that for a child to be capable of thinking beyond a primitive level, his ability to use language was crucial. If Raun did not learn the sounds and words, which are the symbols of things and activities, he would always be glued to the now of his experiences. Symbols would facilitate the development of a system of footnotes from which he could abstract and conceptualize. Without these symbols, Raun's horizons would be limited. It would be like having rooms filled with thousands and thousands of files, but with no labels or index system to retrieve information. Locating a specific dossier would be an improbable, if not impossible, chore. And so it might be for the mind, which contains millions and millions of memory units but has no language shorthand to recall specific data.

We seemed to have been making progress in most areas with the exception of language. We continued our research. More endless phone calls. We talked with speech therapists and language specialists, read books on linguistics, manuals on language development, syntax and semantics. We reviewed details of tongue and muscular coordination of the mouth. Where was the answer? The key was still missing.

An infant walks when he can and when he wants to. He learns to talk when he can and wants to.

Raun did have the facility to mimic sounds and words, although at times there was a strangeness . . . when he would repeat the word in exactly the same tone and voice quality as

95

it was said. There was also the question about his capacity to control his tongue properly. Even so, we knew that, when he wanted to, he could at least approximate words audibly. It was use, not quality, that was important now. The ability was evident in his articulations, but the difficult next step was still heavily dependent on motivation.

Basically, he continued to be echolalic, repeating some of what he had just heard, but never using it with meaning or intent. An enigma. Yet, since imitation was an essential of learning, there was the promise of other possibilities. As before, we wanted to display language in use and form so as to illustrate to Raun the advantages of talking. Leading him to a desire for communications with words was our intent. When he wanted to, he would find a way.

We decided to pursue a promise, to cash in a token given to us by a doctor in one of the teams that had initially seen Raun. She had told us to bring him back at the end of the summer for another evaluation and they would place him in a special school for language development. It was part of a program designed for the needs of children with learning disabilities and behavioral problems.

Tuesday afternoon. Raun, twenty months of age, sat with us in the lobby waiting for the doctors. Raun sat limply in a chair as Suzi used a cookie to establish eye contact and tried to play with him. Next to us, there was a woman in a wheelchair. Two young boys with glassy eyes and dilated pupils stood leaning against the wall. One had his head hanging as if it were a burden too heavy for him. An old lady stared blankly at the wall. Two girls talked incessantly to each other, punctuating their conversation with bursts of laughter.

At the desk, an overweight attendant munched on M & M's while vacantly "yes"ing all those who made inquiries. A harried executive dressed in a black suit came running through and almost knocked the wheelchair and its occupant over. I looked back at Raun. He was unaware of the people, unaware of the activity around him. Another woman entered the lobby, called out our name and asked us to follow her. As the sound of my heels clicked against the cool and almost colorless tile floor, I noticed the irony of a plaque which said THE HEALTH CENTER.

Inside, another waiting room. This one had two chairs, bare

96

walls and no other occupants. Two doctors entered; they both smiled. They wanted to examine Raun alone. Since he seemed perfectly willing to go with them, we nodded our approval.

A social worker appeared, asked us to follow her into another room so that she could do a comprehensive intake interview and family history. Although we had done this once before for this same unit, she asked that we repeat it for her records. She was a pleasant lady who was well into her fifties. Her dress and hair style was appropriate to the day when Pat Boone lullabyed his popcorn songs. She smiled excessively as if to set a mood . . . an amiable cocktail-party façade.

Her questions were the same ones we had been asked over and over again. As we answered in flat tones, she scribbled rapidly across the page, creating her elaborate clinical poetry. An hour passed. The other doctors returned with Raun, who appeared slightly irritable and uncomfortable.

"Please follow us."

Together we all moved into another, larger room. More blank walls, hard plastic chairs and, for something different, a conference table. The Chief of Pediatric Psychiatry sat down quickly, smiled a plaster of paris smile and neatly folded his hands. This was a routine, everyday performance for him. His eyes darted back and forth from us to his associates. His head seemed flattened in the front and back as if it had been compressed in some giant vice. He appeared studious . . . but physically distorted.

His associate, a neuro-psychologist, was a woman in her middle forties whose nose and chin accented an angular face, making her appear aloof. Her eyes blinked continually as she spoke as if they were punctuation marks in her sentences. Her choppy mannerisms even affected her speech. Her tones were polished with a highly professional and authoritarian gloss, but the fullness of her voice was incomplete and her words broke like pieces of glass on the formica table. And yet we felt in her a sincere and abiding concern.

Actually, the chief did most of the talking, addressing Suzi and me together. Yet, in some ways, he might have been talking to a large anonymous audience. The cadence of his speech had the rhythm of a recording. He reiterated all the diagnostic jargon we had heard before. He suggested additional examinations for muscle coordination, for speech and tongue development, for a neurological analysis. Even though this doctor said that our son had some very dramatic developmental problems he still considered Raun too young to help. Perhaps in another year . . . "bring him back when he is two and a half."

The old words and worn expressions danced in my head. What about the promise for help . . . to help us now? That had been our only reason for returning, our only reason for allowing them to put Raun through more testing. They replied that they would like to help us in teaching Raun, but that his age and his current capabilities made it impossible. They did not consider it feasible.

I couldn't understand . . . couldn't grasp it. What were they saying? Were they telling us that he failed to meet their specifications? Because of age and lack of explicit abilities? Why would anything they did for him be conditional?

I was angry, damn angry, but I knew an outburst would not be effective. I filtered my feelings.

I turned to both doctors, keeping my anger under control. Wasn't early intervention considered important in attempts to help these children? I queried them about Lovaas, Delacato, and Kozloff, all of whom had done extensive work in this area and had written numerous books and articles. Neither one of these professionals was familiar with the works of the authors that I had mentioned. Was it possible? Not to be aware of new strides and techniques in training autistic and emotionally-disturbed children . . . not to know about the current research and experimentation being performed in their own field of specialty?

I could not stop thinking that we had been deceived. We had been had. Raun had been had. I was irritated and feeling abused. Even with all we had been through, this morning had been the most frustrating . . . the pomposity of the half answers and the no answers. The more I allowed my mind to reflect on our meeting the more enraged I became.

Suzi took Raun home. In my car, I headed toward the city. I pounded the steering wheel with my fist, looking for release. Finally my choked emotions flowed. My silent sobbing was accentuated by intruding car horns. I was furious, not depressed and not feeling lost. The future of my child and children like him depended on people like these. Over and over again, their hollow phrases whirled in my mind. Those quiet and dignified voices of sympathy. Those soiled and rehearsed smiles. The dramatized sincerity. They were processing us, pushing us through the system, filling a segment of their professional time . . . accounting for themselves. Earning a day's pay.

And this was the best they could do. Why was I so angry? I guess I believed that my anger would be a catalyst in pushing me to change the entire system. Also, I wanted to tell myself how annoyed I was at allowing myself, Suzi and Raun to be taken in again . . . misled and mistreated. Okay, I would continue to do what I could. Okay, the anger did not make a difference, except as a sign to help me get in touch with some beliefs and the corresponding unhappiness. It had only distracted from what I was wanting and what I really cared about.

Back to Raun . . . knowing that we were the best that he could have . . . that our caring, our knowledge and our pursuits had now even exceeded the endeavors of many professionals in the field. We would continue again.

A week later, we were off to one more interview and work-up on Raun. I had spoken in the evening with a doctor whose name was at the end of a list of interconnecting people that began at the University of California, criss-crossed the country to the State University at Stony Brook, from one individual to another, until it reached a sympathetic young doctor. He was the director of a new outpatient program and seemed wholly sympathetic and interested. I reiterated the beginnings of our program and our progress. We believed we were doing well, but our concern was with our lack of progress in the area of language.

He said that he was fascinated and wanted to help if he could. He knew that it was unusual to have a child diagnosed so early and then placed in a program. I explained that the most extreme autistic symptoms had disappeared or were minimal, but that Raun's growth was still very slow and his withdrawal patterns still very evident. He suggested that we bring our son in so that his developmental work-up team could see him and, perhaps, make a contribution.

The building was extremely modern, yet warmed with design. It had huge windows and wood ceilings. This time, we waited alone in a lobby with soft chairs and an air of quiet. We were then ushered into a room with six occupants, all members of their intake team. Each person introduced himself. The atmosphere was warm, cordial and informal. One of the women took Raun outside and played with him. The interview began with the familiar questions and answers that by now seemed stale. Feeling numb, we tried to stay with it . . . to be fresh and alive. We gave our history, Raun's history, medical data and the progress of our program. The doctors were astute and focused, articulate and comprehending.

Then they went on to the series of tests for Raun (blocks, imitation exercises, eye-contact games, concentration themes, pre-linguistic notations, socialization interactions, etc.) All this was filmed on video tape: using machinery hidden on the reverse side of a two-way mirror. Everything was recorded against a Gesell developmental chart which compares the capacity of a tested child with the generalized norms that are statistically appropriate for children of a similar age. Raun's performance was to be measured against a peer group, in the abstract.

After the testing, there was a general diagnosis and commentary. Raun, at twenty months, was functioning with regard to language and socialization at an approximate age level of eight months, or just slightly above. Large motor activity was appropriate to his age level. His play: scattered from eight months to fourteen months. During the testing, Raun explored the toys lethargically and, at times, did spin. Because of his periods of staring, they introduced a new and novel hypothesis: the possibility that Raun was having some abortive or incomplete form of epileptic grand mal seizures.

The doctor was confused by our elation about progress and growth. If it were not for our reports of where Raun had begun, he definitely would predict for Raun a future of global retardation and limited level of ultimate learning with the possibility of no language acquisition. Since many of the autistic symptoms, such as spinning, rocking, no eye contact had abated, they were confused as to a definite diagnosis or prognosis.

One of the doctors also suggested that he was not convinced that intervention really had made a difference . . . that Raun might simply develop in the same way whether we worked with him or not. In fact, he expressed his laissez-faire attitude

100

quite emphatically. Leave Raun alone, or, at least, let up on the intensity of our program. He did not realize that Raun had come this far only because of our intervention. We had allowed ourselves to want more than what was probable. His advice was contrary to all that we knew to be true. He could afford to speculate that perhaps Raun might have developed anyway . . . he could even experiment with his supposition and ride it right out the window. But we couldn't. Raun was not just another patient, another number . . . he was our son.

They spoke of the other services they provided. The younger doctor noted that our level of operation and intervention dramatically exceeded most of what they were doing.

He set up the "home interview" component of the intake procedure for the following Monday. Again, the video tape was used. Although we understood the limited potential for getting more input, we were thankful to have met a professional who really seemed involved and concerned. He had understood the focus on the "now" of our program rather than preoccupations with diagnosis or future predictions. He was also an ardent believer in early intervention. For this doctor that usually meant dealing with a child three years old. To find a program of intervention with a child only slightly older than one-and-a-half was more than just novel . . . it was an opportunity. They would observe us.

The morning came. The program director and his assistant entered our home. Their request: Do things naturally. If Suzi worked with Raun in the bathroom, then do just that. Suzi was more frenzied than usual, as she took Raun's hand and brought him into the bathroom. They sat together on the small floor area in front of the piles of puzzles and toys. The doctor enthusiastically followed with all his equipment and camera. His assistant also came into the room and found a spot for herself against the door, which was closed once everyone was inside. The doctor surveyed the tiny room, looking for his place. It was becoming more and more obvious, the only unoccupied place large enough to accommodate him and his paraphernalia was the cold and uninviting bathtub.

There was no hesitation. The doctor acted oblivious, as if he did this every day. A real trouper, professionally modest, he lifted his robust form over the edge and slid into the cast-iron womb, ignoring his pressed pants, his studious sports jacket, and his dangling tie. As he lay in the tub silently suffering the discomforts of the rack, he set up the camera.

Raun had noticed the intrusion. For a period of time, he just stared into the front of the lens . . . silent, perhaps even catching a fleeting glimpse of his image reflected on the glass. Saturated, he turned away and began to respond to Suzi. The camera rolled.

Suzi went through all the touching exercises, the puzzles, the toys, the musical instruments. Then she put Beethoven's Ninth Symphony on the tape recorder. Aware that Raun was wandering and losing contact, she took out her special jar, held a plastic instrument to her lips and began blowing bubbles. She talked incessantly to him. Touching him. Trying to stimulate him. In some ways, she was camera sensitive and had compressed many of the activities into a short period of time so that they could be recorded on tape.

The captive physician remained stoic in the tub as beads of sweat gathered on his forehead. A humorous image with a glint of self-mockery, it was an unrehearsed scene from some incomprehensible Woody Allen film. The air being used and reused. The temperature was rising with the overhead lights also heating the room. An hour passed. The door opened, expelling the exhausted participants. They were overwhelmed with the performance.

The doctor composed himself. He was bemused, amused, elated and excited. Finally, he began to speak: "An unbelievable experience. Like nothing I have ever seen. Suzi, your energy level and continual nonstop stimulation was incredible. Marvelous for Raun, but also fascinating for me to watch."

He noted that he was very impressed with Raun's apparent happiness and expressed sensitivity to our son's peacefulness. He had not seen the anger and anxieties that were so often present in other children with Raun's disabilities. Even though Raun was essentially unresponsive, the doctor observed that his fleeting interaction seemed meaningful. He encouraged us to continue and talked about methods and techniques. The doctor was warm and verbal. He suggested that we not ask Raun to do more than one chore at a time so as not to confuse him. Nevertheless, he thought that the scope and sophistication of our

102

program far outpaced his project at the children's center. In fact, it was his assessment that at this point he probably had more to learn from us than we did from him. He again marveled at the intensity and thoroughness of our approach, expressing great interest in the novelty of our concepts. He wanted to keep in touch. Departing, he left behind a book on basic skills and basic language. But our reading and our program had already gone beyond the limits of these texts.

The doctor also suggested that we have a routine EEG (neurological brain scan) done on Raun just to touch all bases, even though he believed it would not really tell us anything new.

Our evening brain-picking sessions still revolved around language acquisition. It was our primary focus. Although we all verbalized incessantly when we were with Raun, we knew that there had to be additional methods to illustrate the use and efficacy of language. Our resolution was to make an intense commitment. Find that new direction. Enable him to take the next step. Directions and body identification were to be kept simple . . . we would develop one-word descriptions, one shortened utterance for things, one syllable. "Ba" for bottle. "Wa" for water. "Ju" for juice. We were going to try to convert his crying into the use of words.

His crying had become his prime language, but it was too generalized and vague to build on. We decided when Raun cried we would be attentive, but act confused. Approximate what he wants, but miss the target. Appear perplexed so that he did not feel we were specifically trying to trick him or deprive him. As we keep itemizing all the different things he might be wanting, name each and every one carefully. When we hit it, he will react by stopping his crying. Reinforce recognition by naming the object several times and by being excited and affectionate with Raun for his achievement. If he sees the use of language as more direct and effective, he might choose to use it. Play dumb, but be helpful . . . be loving.

This new approach did not make an easy week for any of us. Raun was crying more and more, but sticking with us until we could finally locate what he wanted. One evening, while we had guests, Raun came into the living room and grabbed my hand and started to pull. I asked him what he wanted. He began to cry and pull even harder. I told him I would come if he told me what he wanted. The crying increased. As I sat on the floor, he pulled at me with a greater intensity. There was such sadness about him. My first impulse was to get up and go with him . . . but I realized it would be self-defeating for both of us. Crying would have to become more and more ineffective in order to precipitate a move toward talking. He let go of my hand and stood there crying hysterically. Then he walked, sobbing, close to me and put his head between my legs. He stood up and leaned his head on my shoulder. I put my arm around him and stroked him. His sobbing finally stopped. He stayed against my chest and shoulder for several minutes with his hands lying limply at his sides.

Then he moved away and took my sleeve. Immediately, he began to cry again. I again asked him what he wanted, that if he told me, I would help him. He cried even more while tugging at me. Somehow, I knew that he was understanding me, but that he was not willing to speak. Now he was hysterical again. He dropped my hand, looked at me through the rainfall from his eyes and laid himself once again against my chest. I comforted him as he stood there limply.

The crying dissipated . . . he disengaged himself, stood up tall and began all over again. Wanting me to do his bidding. Testing me. Wanting me to come with him and trying to see if his pulling was okay. This episode was repeated no less than five times, until Raun lay down exhausted against my leg and fell asleep.

I felt like a boxer who had just gone fifteen rounds . . . drained and fogged. Wanting to go with him, knowing to stay seated. The pulling and pushing inside. The twisting as I watched someone I loved go through a very private hell in order to explore and experiment.

*   *   *

Observations:
- —More social interaction with family members and friends
- —Using crying continually to communicate
- —Initiates much contact by taking someone's hand and showing him what he wants (to go out, to go upstairs, to get water, etc.)
- —Plays more with toys instead of throwing them; pushes cars, rolls tinker toys, investigates with more patience and concentration
- —Now seems at times actually to prefer people to objects. He will leave an empty room to be in one filled with people
- —Repeats much more, although still no effective use of language . . . but his receptive language is increasing. Understands: down, wa (for water), ma-ma, da-da, don't do that, no, more, moo (for cow), ba (for bottle), come here, Bryn, Thea, Nancy, Maire, doggie, nose, head, ear, eye, upstairs, diaper
- —For the first time, cried to eat and to get water
- —Takes your hand and sometimes throws it at what he wants
- —We have locked certain closets in the kitchen so that he would not take things out and hurt himself. When we forget to close one, he takes us over to it and shows us it is open.

No changes:
- —Still spinning objects
- —Still does not cry to get out of the crib

*　　*　　*

We had dinner this evening with Vikki, who had just been interviewed for a job as a resident therapist at one of the progressive hospitals for the so-called "emotionally disturbed" and "brain-damaged" children. She was bursting at the seams,

105

wanting to spit out all that she had heard and seen. Excited and angry, tense and confused, Vikki was speaking in a rambling and slurring manner, just wanting to get it out:

"And then the supervisor of the school program interviewed me ... and, Barry, you don't know what she said ... I mean this woman was responsible for everything ... the program, the input, hiring ... everything. You know what I mean? You're not going to believe this. Oh, God ... I asked her what she thought about autistic children, what they do with them and all, you know, because of Raun—I wanted to know more—and ... it's just outrageous! She said, 'Autistic children, well, they're really crazy. There's not much you can do with them.' Wait, wait ... that's not all ... Then the guidance counselor said, 'What we do with them is just try to at least train them to be good patients, so they aren't any trouble to the institutions they go on to when they leave here at fourteen. We try to get them to maybe wash themselves, feed themselves, and have them toilet trained. If we accomplish that, we're happy. Other than that, there's nothing to be done with them.' Oh, God ... I couldn't believe it. He talked about them like they were animals—useless, hopeless animals. And no matter what I said, he just kept citing case after case to prove his point. Oh, it's so sad; they're all just rotting away there. I wanted to scream at him, 'You don't understand.' Look at Raun—look at him, what he can do and how great he is. Jesus, I could never work there."

She was panting and fuming. Suzi and I watched her sadly, knowing that what she was relating was all too accurate. Just look at the little they've done with all these children. Autistic children are "incurable," so why bother? How terribly sad and wasteful of the lives and gifts of these little people. Vikki caught her breath and rambled on:

"Then I stayed in one of the music and dance-therapy classes to watch this lady that I would supposedly be working for. There were all kinds of kids there with varying problems. I didn't see any kids there doing the things autistic children usually do. But anyway, I was just standing against the wall—'cause they warned me not to do anything to distract the kids—I mean, I might freak them out or something, the way they put it—and anyway, this one little boy walks up to me. ... I mean, he wasn't really little; he was like almost as tall as I am, but he was about twelve . . . and, it was really wild; he said to me, 'Hey, lady, you're sexy . . . ya know, ya gimme a hard-on.' He didn't upset me, of course, but the teacher—wow! She started carrying on and threatening him. Totally ineffective . . . and the entire place turned into a wild circus, a zoo for little kids. The music was blaring. The kids were pushed and pulled all around into different positions and being forced to participate—Incredible, really . . . I'd never do it like that. They got absolutely zero out of it; they couldn't care less, the way it was presented, the way they were treated—God, I mean, do you believe it? You had to see it. Oh, wait . . . after the class, I went to the supervisor and asked her if they taught any of the autistic children music . . . you know, using music and movement. She said, 'Oh, no; they're excluded from the music program because, you know, they love it too much.' I said, 'What do you mean?' And she said, 'Well, if you know autistic children, when they hear music, they get very involved and start rocking and withdrawing. And since that's their problem, we want to break them of this kind of behavior and acting out their repetitive symptoms. So we don't let them in the music program. After all, you have to understand, we try to get them to act more normal, not reinforce wild behavior.' It was really hard to control myself; you know? It took everything in me to stay cool. I asked her why she couldn't use the music in some way to reach them and train them since they love it so much. 'Oh,' she said, I've heard that one before, but it doesn't work . . . take it from me, the way we're doing it is the only way.' "

Vikki's last words created a heavy silence in the room. We had been all drawn in, listening to her monologue. Even Bryn and Thea, who were very attentive to what Vikki was saying, appeared disturbed. Bryn's eyes were glazed. I asked Vikki if I could take notes on her experience and what these people said to her. I told her that maybe one day I might want to tell this to others.

Raun interrupted her response and began to hum. Suzi and Bryn joined him as Thea and Vikki also sounded their participation. I watched for a while, mute and fascinated. The mood was escalating and everyone settled comfortably into their communal embrace. Then, as if drawn by an irresistible calling, I began to sing with them. Harmonies developed. A cadence was estab-

107

lished. Hands banging a primitive beat hypnotically on the table as the volume grew. And grew. I could feel the intensity of my breathing increasing as my voice expanded. The pitch heightened as the tones grew louder, as if sucked from me by the common energy we were all creating. By now, we were all shouting at the top of our lungs. Raun stayed with us as his alert and dazzled eyes jumped from one face to another. The raging earth music went on until, with no apparent signal, we all suddenly stopped, except for Raun. Left singing alone at an incredible volume, he started to smile so broadly, his eyes disappeared. Knowing the difference, he too suddenly stopped. A ten-second vacuum of silence, then we all began to laugh. This music, softer and less regimented, was the nightcap for this day.

*　　*　　*

Suzi and I felt that we all could use a break in our rather elaborate and demanding schedule. We arranged with Nancy to be with Raun all day Saturday. We planned to spend that day with Bryn and Thea . . . at the home of Suzi's sculpture teacher.

As we drove up a long, curving driveway cut through the woods, we came upon a startling three-story structure. An architectonic metaphor made from cement forms . . . a light-hearted and playful creation with great majesty. Poking their heads out of the convertible, Bryn and Thea gaped at this huge form with open mouths. Further along into the parking area, the girls immediately spotted another elephant . . . smaller with a wooden nose that was designed to be a swing. They both lunged from the car to participate in this piece of living sculpture. On our right were two reclining figures carved in marble. In front of us was an enormous mystic and godlike face cut into a rare prehistoric stone.

And then, through the doorway, we could see another rare piece; Alfred Van Loen, the creator of all this abundance. History and time had carved their marks in the deep crevices that stretched across his forehead and down toward his mouth. A large prominent nose partitioned his dancing luminous eyes. A tall, lean and bearded pre-Christian figure walking the earth in the twentieth century. A veteran of the concentration camps of Nazi Germany, who rose from the dead to be with us now, to

108

express and re-create in wood and stone, in lucite and metal. As he spoke, I heard the echoes of a thousand years in his voice. His large hands grasped mine as he smiled at us and yelled his greeting to the children. Alfred obviously enjoyed their delights and musical chatter.

Alfred gave us and the girls an intimate and very personal tour into his bountiful world of sculpture and treasure, Bryn and Thea shouting and jumping each time they found a recognizable form or figure in his pieces. The many periods and the evolution of his style merged into this one experience. His classical and more lyrical period had given way to his impressionistic and abstract exploration of form. His insistence on wanting the raw stone or rock to give him the answer . . . to find within and uncover the essence that is there. His belief that each uncut or uncarved piece of wood or marble or onyx had inherent qualities that would suggest its ultimate form and content. His approach was parallel to our approach with Raun, and his pieces reflected that sensitivity and respect.

Passing from one studio area to another, he described the how and what of his art. Each piece of sculpture was a sumptuous story of mood and feelings with its historical footnotes and personal notations. A beautiful opening of a man for others to see and experience . . . going beyond his decades of external manifestations into the deep ravines to share his wealth with us. Suzi was excited and touched by his greeting, his caring and giving us his time. I was intoxicated and almost overloaded by the dazzling visual display and those multicolored, multifaceted stories. I was aware of missing Raun, wanting him to be here . . . daydreaming about returning with him one day to share in this abundance.

We drank coffee with Alfred, who was joined by his young son, Noah. We sat watching the birds dart around the bird feeder. Later, we shared a walk in his garden. More hours back in the studio as we wandered through again and again, thirsty for more, but never satiated.

On this day, we spent time with a master whose talents and humanity far exceed the immediate reaches of his art. A sculptor whose deep and dramatic pieces move from the volcanic to the lyrical and amusing. They cry and sing, make statements and laugh. We departed with a new wealth . . . and a special gift

109

born directly from his fingertips . . . a pen-and-ink drawing. We decided to save it in order to re-present it on another day to Raun . . . whose beauty and soulfulness had also been with us on this day.

That evening, at home, still high on the day's excitement, we built another fire and ate dinner together on the floor in front of the flames. Raun and Nancy joined us. We were together in loving silence as the music of John Coltrane and Keith Jarrett filled the room.

Eight

Suddenly one week Raun stopped working in his sessions. He refused to participate; would not do the puzzles or turn the pages in the books. He began to throw everything again and cry for no apparent reason. He also stopped paying attention when spoken to; he would even turn his back on Suzi or Nancy when they spoke to him. He was ignoring them and making sure they knew it, with heavy and loud notes of defiance.

Even outside the sessions, Raun was changing. One day had now become three. We began noting some loss of eye contact and a mild return to spinning and rocking. Also, Raun did not solicit physical contact. Often, although not all the time, he refused to be touched. Yet he was still in contact . . . when he wanted something, he would still take our hands to direct us. Or move us for his own ends.

One minute rejecting us, then the next playful. Moody. Erratic and unpredictable.

What was happening? What was our son trying to tell us with his behavior? In part, he could have been protesting our feigning ignorance when he cried to get what he wanted. Maybe, more precisely, he was saturated for the moment. Maybe he had decided for the first time that he wanted a change—a slow-

111

down—and was doing his best to let us know. To precipitate a turn in the direction.

Okay, we wanted to be responsive. Immediately, we cut his structured session from six hours a day to two hours. The remainder of the time was used for random stimulation, contact and play time with him as the director, a position which he assumed most of the time. He was stronger and more capable. After several days, he began to come around. He seemed happier and more excited.

We kept the sessions to a minimum, while making them a little more demanding. We were more emphatic about our requests. He accepted this, since outside of the workroom he was the "king" and he knew it. A balance. Since I believe Raun was feeling that he was losing control, this was an acceptable way to re-establish it. His protest was his form of manipulation. And, in this apparent movement backward, we all went forward together.

It remained a difficult week for Raun. He was still crying to communicate . . . a pattern that seemed to have become indelible. Not getting what he wanted quickly. Periods of confusion and frustration, even anger. We stayed with it, and not surprisingly, so did he. Knowing that he could go on . . . that each major step was big and difficult as was each step before. He was propelled, not by us, but by his desire for a more-responsive environment. The crying almost at a tantrum level all the time, filling the house with its shrill dissonance. We stayed soft, helpful and caring. It was very difficult and exhausting.

Raun was standing by the sink crying. Suzi talked to him. Showing him the spoon, then a fork, then the sponge and finally an empty glass. Raun, each time, reacting by crying more. He was not satisfied. Finally, she would fill the glass with water and give it to him. As he settled down, Suzi would say:

"Water, Raun. Here's 'wa.' Say 'wa,' Raun. Here it is, 'wa.' "

Raun gulped it down. Later in the day, he returned to the same spot and started the same procedure over. Suzi went through her usual confusion. Raun persisted. The intensity of his crying grew. Suzi kneeling, loving and solicitous as she watched him twist his face and push at his lips.

"What do you want, Raun? What do you want? Tell me." And then, from the very depths of his body, tearing through his

112

vocal cords to make a sound, twitching his eyes as if he were harnessing all the strength and the power in him. Bellowing in a clear and loud voice, filling the room, Raun shouted:

"WA."

Suzi jumped to her feet, quickly filled the glass and gave it to him. Her hands were shaking as she said: "Yes, Raun. Wa. Wa, Raun. You're such a good boy."

A stunned little man . . . even he seemed surprised. As he gulped down the water, he peered up at his mother with his huge brown eyes as she gently touched his hair.

Hurrah! Raun had done it. He had said a word. Precisely. With intent and meaning. Like wildfire, the word spread. Suzi called me at the office, then called Nancy, then Maire and Steve and Marv and Vikki and Rhoda. Our elation was intense. When Bryn heard the news, she jumped up and down, cheering at the dumbfounded center of attraction. Thea giggled and ran to Raun with open arms. Spread the word, like Henny Penny telling everyone that the sky is falling. The ice had melted, freeing the voice that had once been frozen and inaccessible.

The exercise was repeated at the sink by Raun. First, he started by crying, then became angry as Suzi tried to help him with her fumbling. After a short period of time, he said it again: "WA."

Suzi immediately rewarded him. Raun's short, twisted first word was the first step in a new series of possibilities. Perhaps this was the birth of another dimension.

At dinner, after Raun had finished eating, he looked directly at Suzi and said: "Down."

Beautiful and clear. Spoken with such authority. The word that he had heard thousands of times when he was lifted down from his chair now came freely from his lips. Immediately, we grabbed him and put him on the floor. Later, after Suzi had given him some juice, he held the empty glass up to her and said: "More."

The gushing of words from the dam. It's as if he had been pregnant with them for so many weeks and today was giving birth. On the way upstairs to bed, he said his fourth word for the day . . . all new to his virgin throat and new to our receptive ears.

"Ba," he said, indicating the verbal shortcut for his bottle.

113

That day ended with four giant steps . . . four words.

To celebrate, the next morning, we took Bryn, Thea and Raun to an amusement park. Everyone, including Raun, was in excellent spirits and excited. Our mood was rich and high—champagne and caviar. The desserts were the roller-coaster, the ferris wheel, the whip and the merry-go-round.

First we put the girls on the roller-coaster, deciding to place Raun on something more docile and conservative. We put his little form into the seat of a miniature car which went around in a circle. This would be his first ride. He loved it like a trouper, grinning as the car moved. The girls then wanted to take him on the ferris wheel. Since it moved slowly and without sharp jerks, we agreed. The three of them were put into the wire cage. Up, up and up. Around and down. Standing on the pavement and waving to our crew. They all seemed so happy. Thea taking Raun's hand and waving it each time they passed. Raun was dazzled and smiling. And Bryn kept saying: "Say 'hi.' Say it, Raun. Say 'hi.'"

On to the merry-go-round, each of the girls was strapped on top of a moving horse. Wooden figures carved thirty years ago with bulging eyes and garish paint. Old nickelodeon music poured out from an ancient music box. We stood next to Raun, holding him even though he was strapped onto his horse, not wanting him to be left alone as the platform went round and round. It started to move slowly. As it gathered speed, Raun looked around wildly and began to laugh. He loved it. The girls shouted their hellos to him as they bounced up and down on their mechanical saddles.

When the ride ended, Bryn and Thea wanted to go back on the roller-coaster. This time, they wanted to take their brother. Suzi and I debated for several minutes, and after considering Raun's reaction to the other rides, it seemed reasonable. We tucked the three of them under the bar in the first car. Slowly, the small train moved up the ramp and then let loose on the tracks. We positioned ourselves at the part of the ride where the cars come rushing by at ground level, and waited.

I chewed on my lips to distract myself. Finally, they came into view. Bryn and Thea both had their arms around him . . . he sat between them in the seat. He was wide-eyed. Although he did not seem to be afraid, we weren't quite sure he was enjoying

114

himself. The car speeding by with Bryn and Thea waving frantically. Up the ramp and back down the worn tracks with their short and furious drops, their sharp and twisting curves. Again the train came into view. This time, Raun was laughing with the girls.

A cotton-candy image of children enjoying being alive, loving their experiences and sharing their companionship. Our children so very touched by each other and their common excitement. Joined in this carnival world of metallic dreams and playland fantasies. And for Raun specifically it was a special treat of the motion and speed with which he was so often preoccupied. His fascination momentarily satiated by this plunge into a mechanized whirlpool.

*　　*　　*

Another week passed. Raun was elated and in great spirits. On and off, he was using his three or four words, but with no consistent regularity. Bryn and Thea were enjoying him more . . . instead of being only teachers, they were becoming true playmates. Friends. For another family, Raun's interaction might still be judged as minimal and distant. For us, it was light-years from the beginning. Raun . . . an involving and now involved person.

Following his increased capacity to concentrate, we decided to venture out of the bathroom and into the den. He had become sufficiently expert with his games and interaction, so that we believed he could tolerate more distraction. A slow reintroduction into a more realistic and natural environment. A room with windows. Walls with paintings and photographs. Shelves with books and records. A floor covered by a rug.

We bought him a little chair and used a hassock from one of our large chairs as his table. He was perfectly content in his new environment. In fact, he did not seem at all distracted. He would spend several minutes investigating the room upon entering, but then returned his attention to Suzi and the games.

We began another phase. Direct imitation games originating with the teacher. Touch your nose. Clap your hands. Point to your eyes. Shake your head. Each time he was shown and asked to do it, he would follow. He worked well with photographs and was able to point to various people on request. His interest in puzzles seemed to be waning, so we continued to use food as a stimulant and a reward to induce him to work with the puzzles. We also interjected more physical game playing back into the program. This physical contact began to become a secondary reward for him . . . the tickling, the peekaboo, the being thrown in the air and the jumping. The smiles and laughs came with greater frequency and regularity. Each day passed with a new openness for loving and fun.

Fun . . . somehow that was it. He was enjoying himself more. Enjoying the games and involvement more. Enjoying us more. Raun was freer with himself and with his affection. Even his eyes seemed to talk, to communicate subtleties of feelings and fondness. His interest in being with other children in the park also had increased. More engaging. More solicitous of playtime with his sisters. More joyful in his responses. This characterized only a portion of his behavior . . . but it was this portion that was growing each day.

The self-stimulating activities continued, yet on a more limited basis. Raun still spun and did so at times for extended periods. He still drifted off by himself and became locked in his distant and encapsulated world. Although often in contact, he still spent the equivalent of about three to three and a half hours out of touch . . . staring, rocking, spinning. During the other ten hours, we were able to maintain a fairly continued and rich contact.

* * *

LOG: THE FOURTEENTH WEEK

Observations:
  —In contact with family members for periods of ten to fifteen minutes at a time, quality of contact excellent in reference to eye contact and acceptance of physical interaction
  —Note more interest in push and pull toys
  —Responds more quickly to calls and requests . . . more alert and more receptive to audio

116

—Babbles now (sounds like his own language, not really an approximation of words); when he seems puzzled or frustrated, when he is trying to move something that does not seem to move easily, he will mumble to himself
—More pointing to pictures with interest . . . now even seems to have noticed paintings and photographs on the walls around the house
—Still speaking those four words he began to use last week . . . no new acquisition of language beyond this point
—Have become aware of a very specific and repetitive tune that he sings to himself now . . . over and over.

No changes:
—Still spinning and rocking
—Still easy for him to be by himself for long periods of time Will go off and sit in one spot as if meditating, but will respond to our intervention and will interact with us

Notes:
—Notice an increasing interest in music, not only the tapes . . . but now spends time with Suzi exploring the notes and sounds on the piano. Also increased interest in the drums, tambourines, flutes used in his sessions
—Although he has remained confined to using only four words, we noted if we say the word to him in a low voice, he copies not only the word, but the actual tone in which it was said. Also noted that he often works his mouth and tongue in a disjointed and irregular manner . . . as if they were not fully under his control or he did not know how to correctly utilize them

*   *   *

The pervasive nature of our involvement with Raun and its many amplifications had curtailed my involvement with my horse and the pleasures of horseback riding. Aware of wanting more contact with this sport, I decided to spend an entire Saturday in the saddle, from sunrise to sunset instead of the usual limited three-hour outing. To be with nature, with the wind, and Kahlil.

An ironic twist . . . in my having given my horse and my son a common name. Framed in poetry. Both of them set apart and different. A year before Raun was born, I had purchased Kahlil, a four-year-old appaloosa gelding with a high spirit and dramatic appearance. His ancestors were painted on the walls of the Pharaohs' tombs in the recesses of the Pyramids. Considered by some to be the oldest breed on the face of the earth. In this country, the appaloosa traces back to before the Nez Percé Indians. A horse known for its athletic build, driving spirit and sensitive swiftness. The wind blew inside of Kahlil. A rush of electrical excitement.

This was not just another horse . . . he was very large, an imposing animal with the rare "watch eye." His left eye was that of a normal horse, brown and deep. His right eye, the "watch eye," had a light blue iris set in a wide field of white . . . a duplication of a human eye. Eerie. Mystical. The Indians considered a horse with a watch eye to be possessed by the gods. Our more modern society calls it an imperfection which supposedly often characterizes a more skittish and unpredictable animal. In some stables, an imperfect horse such as Kahlil would be destroyed to maintain the purity and quality of the line. A blind and conceptual approach to differences. It was this beautiful mark of difference that was this horse's specialness.

Once he was harnessed, I found in Kahlil more than I had ever imagined . . . a lightning spirit and old soul character . . . with the freedom and daring to live energetically in the springtime of his life. Consistent with nature. And now, how odd and foreboding, to find much of this horse in my special son. Like this statuesque animal, Raun too had a profound beauty that others judged problematic and wanted to discard. Parallels.

When I bought him, Kahlil was barely saddle broken. His only decided and obvious talent was his capacity to go forward at great speeds. Although I was not an accomplished rider, I had decided to train him myself. To train him as I learned. I wanted to have that experience with him. Eighteen books later, I mounted my horse. Every weekend and several evenings each week. We began slowly and with great difficulty. Even the stable owner and his wife, who helped me, felt Kahlil was a difficult and different animal, but with heart and sensitivity.

Many times, it would take all my strength just to hold him from bolting ahead. Often, because of his erratic and unpredictable behavior, I found myself on the ground. On one occasion, he tossed me over his head at a full gallop. I fell in front of his legs, but he carefully jumped high into the air to avoid trampling me. An enigmatic, but caring relationship had been formed.

We both survived each other during this initial training period and together we graduated to jumping. First, only very small logs. Then, small fences, and larger ones. Finally, soaring over the hood of an old red Volkswagen. But, before we developed this degree of perfection, Kahlil had thrown me fourteen times in our joint movements into the air. At times, he would stop just short of a jump . . . stop dead without warning and flip me head over heels to the ground. Often, he would make a sharp, unsolicited turn as his front legs hit the ground after taking a jump. Usually, this threw me off balance and off his back.

Finally, a year had passed and we were still together. An odd couple. We both had more excitement and stamina than style. We learned to move as one, to respect each other. Others in the stable found Kahlil difficult to ride. He had moods and seasons. A sensitive apparition whose humanoid eye created a sense of imbalance in all who caught his gaze. They saw not his beauty but their own discomfort. Yet, for me, he was a friend. His wildness was the beauty of his special spirit. Like Raun, a gift for those who would know him.

By six in the morning we were on the trails . . . moving swiftly across the wet grass still bathed in the slick and sparkle of the morning dew. Kahlil was in great spirits. My hands already felt the continual pressure of holding him back. As we reached an open field where the ground had dried in dawning sun, I relaxed my grip on the reins, knowing there was a better footing for his surging ahead. Sensing the freedom, Kahlil immediately began to lunge forward into a full run, almost flying across the expanse. Our bodies moved together as one, gliding over the surface of the earth. I cheered him as he moved through the white light of his speed. Then we eased back into a slow canter, then a trot and finally drifted into an easy walk through the tall grass beside a majestic pine forest. In the afternoon, I stopped by the neglected ruins of the old estate. Eating and talking to my horse. My chatter answered by his snorts. Yet, in the singularity of our joint venture, I felt a sincere and solid affection. Grinding grass with his teeth as he eyed me. Rubbing his hoof in the grass. Staying with me without being fatigued. Kahlil was an old soul, a comrade in our excursions into speed and flight.

As the sun began to move behind the trees, we headed back toward the stable. He pulled again, wanting to be let loose before returning. I obliged. For fifteen minutes he flew through the woods, across tight, winding trails and over stone fences from another century. His body created a soft white lather as his lungs drew deep and throaty gallons of air. My ears were caressed by the rising pitch of the winds; my limbs feeling connected with all that's alive.

Later, slowing down for the long walk back. To cool him . . . to rest him . . . to be with him and myself. Kahlil had given me a beautiful day. The click of his shoes on the hard earth, the soft panting and the surflike sound of the winds created a quiet harmony. My horse and I. Primitive. Pure. Our relationship elemental. What initially appeared to be difficult and problematic had developed into a profound respect and attachment. Echoes of Raun.

Nine

Now that our little boy was capable of absorbing more and more with each passing day, we kept trying not only to vary the program, but also to introduce new areas and concepts of working. The motivational aspect of the program had been developed extensively and was now giving way to slightly more sophisticated educational and skill-teaching exercises and games.

Raun was propelled from within. He initiated a major portion of the contact in all his sessions. During the times when he withdrew or became preoccupied, we would revert to utilizing food as a stimulus.

In many instances, we would use secondary pleasures as a vehicle for his involvement. For example, if he liked to jump or be tickled or go outside, we would suggest one of these activities to him. If he responded, we interjected another exercise between his desire and the object or activity we desired. He could then decide as to whether it was worthwhile to involve himself. Most often, he would immediately begin to participate. Occasionally, he would remain aloof. Emphatically. And this statement of independence would always be respected.

Suzi and Nancy thought of another developmental work concept. They both agreed that water was an excellent tool to develop increased sensory awareness and an environmental tool in which physical contact could be promoted and enjoyed. The novelty . . . sessions in the bathtub.

Nancy would set aside periods of time for this project. After the initial exposures, Raun began to settle easily into the water. They began. Games feeling the water. Drinking the water. Sprinkling and splashing the water. Nancy putting water in her hands and wetting his hair. Then, inviting him to do the same. Touching was also an important activity factor. He seemed delighted in the awareness of himself.

Most children are continually in diapers, clothing and shoes. They never have much of an opportunity to come to know their bodies at an early age. It was this exploration that helped Raun solidify a more specific and definite concept of "me." Although not articulated in language, he better sensed his physical perimeters and explored the space around him. A new toy that was himself. Sometimes for ten or fifteen minutes he would rub his fingers slowly and gently across his belly. Alert and inquisitive.

Raun was now not only using those few words he had acquired, but was starting to learn new ones. It moved very slowly. After tremendous prodding and encouragement, he finally began to use the words "Mommy," "Da-da," and "hot." This brought his total vocabulary to seven words. The other words, which included, "ba," "wa," "out" and "down," were being used with greater frequency and more regularity. They were easily incorporated into his normal repertoire of behavior. They were his wheels, they provided him with mobility.

This morning, Raun ran from his crib directly to the piano, which is just outside his bedroom. An old upright which must have celebrated those earlier years before the existence of television. Suzi was with him as his fingers glided at random over the keys. At first . . . softly. Then, bursting with energy, he slammed down the white keys with great bravado. He then suddenly stopped. He had just noted the black keys . . . an area of the keyboard he had always neglected. First, he touched only one of them, running his index finger across the top and exploring the side which rises above the sea of white keys. He smiled as if he had made some internal realization.

Suzi found herself smiling too. She knew to leave him to his new discoveries. He still made contact and showed his awareness of her. He'd turn, cock his head to the side and look directly into Suzi's eyes. She would smile at him and he would return the smile.

A half hour passed before he lost interest and became sluggish. Suzi decided to intervene. She played a sequence of three notes . . . the first three notes of "Three Blind Mice." Raun watched and listened. She played it again. And again. Still he watched and sat very still. Taking one of his fingers in her hand, she touched it to each note in the same cadence she had played them. She repeated this several times. He remained passive. Then Suzi returned to playing the notes by herself. Raun looked at her again, paused and very cautiously placed his fingers on the keys. One, two, three. A note for each of the mice. He did it in the exact way he had heard it. Then he mimicked the sequence with other notes. Suzi answered each of his efforts with her piano flourish . . . "Three Blind Mice." He repeated each time. Hands moving across the keyboard. A mother and her child, experimenting, imitating, enjoying. Loving each other. They were like the wind moving through the air . . . so much a part of each other.

* * *

One warm Sunday morning, we tumbled our family into the car and headed for the shore. Taking blankets, towels, bathing suits, balls, shovels, pails and a kite.

Raun was walking, crawling and falling in the sand at the beach. Alert and comical, he played with Bryn and Thea as they built their castles in the sand. His feet marched over their fantasy skyscrapers, destroying their bridges and collapsing the streets of their make-believe cities. But laughingly they made a game of rebuilding, while pretending Raun was their Godzilla.

I took his shoes off. For several minutes, he seemed hesitant to take a step. Walking on this kind of surface in bare feet was a new experience for him. He began on his tiptoes in an effort to balance and secure himself which landed him on his face. I helped him to his feet and went through the motions with him. A bit of practice and he moved about by himself. Then down to the surf, watching the small waves from a distance. I held him

123

dangling above the water, just letting his feet dip in. The bite of its cool surface. He pushed upward. Held his feet high for a few seconds and then he ventured to put them back in the water by himself. He stayed with it for almost an hour.

The sun began to wane and we gathered our crew back to the blanket to watch the sunset. Suzi, Bryn, Thea and I cuddled together. I got up and brought Raun back to the blanket. He stayed only for a few seconds and then walked off, intermittently joining us and wandering away. Testing. Coming and going in a further exploration of his freedom and space. And our acceptance.

At home, he seemed to become bored over the next three days. His behavior patterns seemed slightly more infantile. The little achievements that used to occur each day ceased to be obvious. He was treading water, biding his time.

Our immediate response was once more to loosen the program . . . exchanging hours of his work sessions for more random, unstructured play. We also noticed he was losing the joy and playfulness that he had exhibited in physical-contact games. He was choosing more and more to be by himself. Raun was moving away. Everyone was sensitive to it. The awareness was infiltrating our mood. Something was changing. An alteration of the spark. A new sluggishness . . . an obvious movement away from people.

Suzi, Marie, Nancy and I, joined together in more nightly conferences. Additional discussions between Suzi and me. We spent hours talking . . . conversations that consumed entire nights as we exchanged observations. Trying to be more alert to Raun and the messages that were implicit in his behavior.

There was an escalation in his outbursts. Raun had started to throw over the furniture in the house. We allowed it, thinking it would probably pass. Unfortunately, he stepped up his attacks on the chairs and the couch. Now he was causing damage. We decided to introduce verbal disapproval for the first time. Each time he threw something over, we responded in a heavy tone saying, "No!" It didn't seem to help. In fact, our scolding him actually fueled the flames. Attention. Wanting and getting attention . . . focusing our behavior. Raun was controlling the situation and, I guess, getting what he wanted. But we were not.

124

Our responses reinforced what he was doing. We had hardly ever used this as a method, and each time we did, it slapped us in the face like a rifle backfiring. There were also other signs we began to notice. He would continue to do his routine as we scolded him. We would also catch him smiling as he completed the act. Raun had set in motion a pattern to control us and we had been sucked in. Compatriots and partners.

As a survival alternative, for the furniture and for Raun, every light piece of furniture that was easy for him to overturn was removed to the garage. By doing this we accomplished two things. We saved our furniture and we removed the causal factor for using disapproval as a technique. Raun was very concerned about the missing items for almost a week. He was unsure of the change.

Now he was becoming even more unruly and unwilling to cooperate in his sessions. He was now refusing to do exactly what he had cherished just weeks ago. We slowed down the program even more. There were longer periods of unstructured play. We watched him for the cues. For the signs.

LOG: SIXTEENTH WEEK

Observations:

—Bathroom sessions in the bathtub with Nancy and Raun continue productively

—Raun withdrawing; uncooperative, unruly, pushing over furniture

—Still speaking his very limited vocabulary of water, bottle, down, hot, out, Mommy and more. Will no longer use words if asked directly

—Still very involved in music. Hums to himself, moves his body to music without being told or requested to do so. Sat with Suzi ten minutes and listened to Beethoven's Fifth Piano Concerto

—Laughs when he is doing something he believes we don't want him to do

—Relates easily to pictures . . . points to people and things
when asked

No changes:
—Spinning and rocking continue
—Still aloof and socially withdrawn

*　　*　　*

His moods became more erratic. His behavior was often
punctuated with periods of unruliness. All of this continued for
weeks. His actual work sessions were limited to about three and
a half hours each day, less than half of what they had been
previously. The remainder of the time was spent in supervised
free play, during which Raun always set the pace and place,
designed the activity and controlled the interaction.

The more we relaxed and altered the program, the more his
mood softened. He was responding. Perhaps he had taught us
something again and now had no need to continue his antics
and contrary behavior. Conceivably, this might have been
Raun's method of reaching us . . . to communicate his desire to
pull back and move us to change the schedule so that he might
have the opportunity to pause. The more we reacted to his cue,
the more he responded to us.

We were excited by the effected changes. But then the gloss
wore thin. He began to push against even the abbreviated sessions. A darkness was coming over him that we did not understand. A retreat. Our son seemed alienated and more distant.
Less sensitive to hearing and visual stimuli.

The drooling from his mouth became more prominent. His
tongue was less in his control. His eyes frozen. Was he physically
ill? Were these signs of the flu or a cold? After a medical check-
up, Raun was confirmed as a healthy physical specimen with a
very minor sore throat. But perhaps "minor" is a heavy burden
on his system . . . maybe it takes less to cut his wires and stop
his functioning. We had noticed that whenever he was ill, even
slightly, there was always some sort of altered state or "apparent regression."

When he put a piece of the puzzle into its respective spot, he would pause, holding the section in the air for several minutes . . . staring at it. Contemplating. The space between his movements was reminiscent of his behavior of four months ago. We also noted a lag between our verbal requests and his acting upon them. Connection again seemed to be a question. Once he could focus, he moved in an alert and determined fashion. Somehow, Suzi suspected that he himself was blocking the circuitry, giving himself more time to decide whether he wanted to push himself—to expend the extra effort necessary to move ahead.

In some way, this twenty-two-month-old individual was reviewing himself . . . trying to decide whether to go on . . . weighing his knowledge, his reasons and his evidence. We considered all the questions he might be asking himself. But the almost mute world he occupied precluded us from intervening or from helping. Even the intensity and frequency of his crying had been stepped up as he started to discontinue using words. His face was more fixed and rigid in expression. His body was more staccato and mechanical in its movements. Even the stars in his eyes were dull.

I watched him, feeling confused and helpless as he began to position his fingers by his lips and flap them. Raun was changing and our roller-coaster life was taking another turn.

*   *   *

LOG: EIGHTEENTH WEEK—LOOSE SCHEDULE

Observations:
   —Diminishing use of effective language, although responsive to language
   —Avoiding physical contact and fondling
   —More mouthing; rolling his tongue back and forth, and sucking on his lips
   —Often wants to go upstairs to be alone; does not solicit company or companionship

—No rocking this week

—Some playing with toys by himself and scattered interaction with the family

No changes:

—His fixation on spinning objects

—Moving away from social contact.

* * *

There was a growing tension in the house. Everyone was working with Raun, extending huge amounts of permissiveness. Yet we seemed to be losing him. Each day, his temperament became more erratic. More unpredictable. Sometimes he worked well and then, at other times, he was very uncooperative . . . as if he were testing us. We allowed it. Permitted him his deviance and withdrawal.

Yet his withdrawal grew more severe as if some spreading cancer threatened to extinguish him and all that we had accomplished. The isms began to reappear with increased intensity . . . more rocking, spinning and staring, more avoidance of physical contact and pushing us away. Raun's crying had expanded into almost every waking hour. The entire program had become almost nonfunctional.

Then it happened . . . Saturday morning. Suzi took Raun out of the crib and noticed his aloof and serious demeanor. She took him down into the kitchen and went to fetch the other children. From the bedroom, I heard the top of a metal can hissing its way across the floor. Raun was spinning . . . it went on incessantly. I found myself transfixed by the sound. Waiting. Finally, while in the middle of shaving and trimming my beard, I decided to interrupt myself. To see if I could interest Raun in something else . . . wondering where everyone was . . . sensing that Raun was alone.

As I entered the kitchen, Suzi was standing motionless against one of the cabinets, staring glassy-eyed at the little boy in the center of the floor. Bryn and Thea watched silently from their seats at the table and felt the uneasiness. Raun was extremely busy and involved . . . each time he got the top going, he stood

128

up on his tiptoes, bent over the twirling object and flexed his hands in a strangely jerking and irregular pattern. We had not seen this kind of behavior in over four months. It was like being back at the beginning. A nightmare played out before our hesitant eyes.

I sat next to my son and quietly called his name. No answer. I said his name louder. Again, no answer. Deaf? No audio? It couldn't be. I grabbed a book from the counter and slapped it against my hand only five inches from his head. Not a single twitch in his eyelids. No evidence of the noise in any part of his body. Not the slightest movement.

As he continued to spin, I waved my hand in front of his eyes. No blinking. I snapped my fingers, almost hitting his face. No response . . . no recognition of intake, except that he was intently fixed on the spinning object.

I rose from the floor, feeling the pulse of my life drained from me. Gone. Here and yet gone from us. Avoiding Suzi's eyes, I suggested we all have breakfast together.

Suzi went over to Raun to pick him up, but he resisted by making his body stiff and by pushing her away with his hands. She came over to the table alone. Our meal was eaten in a pensive silence as Raun kept up his bizarre and intricate pantomime only four feet from the table. We continually offered him food and waited until he found himself wanting it.

What to do? Go back, back to the very beginning. Intervene with food. Gently. Sit with him. Imitate him. Approve of him and his activities.

It could have been easy . . . we had all been through it many times. Elementary and yet it was not. We had first to assess our feelings, consider what we were believing. Was our loving and feeling good about Raun contingent on his progressing and achieving? Did we expect a guarantee that this forward movement would continue, that he would always keep improving and never return to his original autistic state? And were we now thinking that this day marked the end? That it had all been in vain? That we had lost him behind that invisible and impenetrable wall? Suzi and I worked through all these beliefs and feelings. We could really know nothing for sure. We could only love him and keep going. Through it all, we knew that this was a time for Raun to be with himself. Perhaps to return to what now had become a former way of existing, a previous life.

He seemed to be going through a strange and melancholy dialogue with himself. As if he were deciding whether to stay with his present accomplishments, go back to old behaviors, or push ahead into an even more unknown and, perhaps, difficult world.

Adjust everything. Go all the way back. First, we told Nancy, then Maire. They were tense and confused . . . but accepting. They both wanted to do what would be best for Raun. Maire had the first afternoon shift. Suzi was in the living room with a friend. From the corner of her eye, she noticed Maire standing in the doorway. Suzi asked if everything was okay. Maire nodded her head. Affirmative. Minutes later, Suzi realized that Maire was still in exactly the same position, leaning against the door. Her hands were cupped over her eyes. Suzi moved out of the chair and went to her. Lowering her hand, Maire exposed the stream of tears flowing down her face.

"What's the matter, Maire? What's wrong?"

"I can't stand it. I love him so much and to see him like this after all the progress just kills me."

Suzi hugged her until she finished crying.

"Come on, Maire, let's sit down and talk about it. About Raun."

Maire felt that what was transpiring was terrible . . . irreversible. That, in many ways, she had expected him to keep getting better, to keep improving. That, in loving him, she had found herself needing him to be healthy and involved. She understood the trap that she had created . . . she understood her unhappiness. It would not be okay to lose him. And yet, precisely because it was not okay, she understood that, in some way, she was now disapproving of his behavior . . . and, ultimately, that would lead to disapproving of him. She wanted to feel good about his supposed regression . . . to allow him this slide backward (or forward) into the autistic womb. She knew, as we had all come to learn that, if we had expectations of him, we set ourselves up for directing him toward specific goals and for creating our own disappointments. What about our concepts of no judgments and no expectations? They again explored the Attitude: "To love is to be happy with." And if this was it—for Raun and the ultimate design of his world, couldn't all of us feel good about what we

130

have had? About the gift of experiencing the life of this little boy?

There were no promises. Just today. Maire looked into Suzi's eyes and managed a half smile. Her dedication and her concern were so intense that sometimes it was a problem to her. She was learning to love more freely. Maire called out Raun's name and returned to her student.

We worked through the same questions with Nancy. With Bryn and Thea. And back to the courts for us . . . throwing the new reality to each other until we could both field it. Again and again. There was no way of knowing. There was just the wanting and the doing. Pushing the probable. Be with him. Love him. Be happy with him . . . wherever he was.

* * *

The program reverted to the very first stage. We strove for intense communication of our approval and loving; trying to motivate him again and to tap his wanting. Each morning and afternoon were like a replay of the summer. Maire and Nancy were now accustomed to the reversal. Suzi and I were accepting, sensing that Raun was perhaps still deciding. Suzi became more positive; hypothesizing that he was contemplating who he was and where he was.

* * *

The ninth day after Raun's withdrawal. Early morning. Suzi went to his crib to bring him to breakfast. As she entered his room, he was humming. When she appeared beside his bed, he looked directly at her. After absolutely no eye contact for over a week, she was elated and overjoyed. She touched his cheek with her hand and he didn't pull away. She put her lips gently against his opened hand and kissed him. He grabbed her nose. Suzi laughed and began to tickle him as he lay down giggling. Suzi's laughter suddenly turned into loud and heavy sobbing.

From the den, I was startled by the sounds. Jumping out of the chair and flying up the steps, I fought against my mind's picture of the nightmare that could correspond with Suzi's crying. As I entered the room, she was holding Raun in her arms

131

and walking back and forth across the room. Touching his hair and rubbing his back. He was incredibly alert. As I watched, he began to imitate her sad face. I knew what had happened. Raun was back with us. Our little man had returned from his twilight land of in-between.

We brought him into our bedroom. His mood was definitely cheerful. As soon as I sat on the bed, he came over to me, seeking my hands. Smiling at him, I helped him up and then tossed him into the air. He began to laugh and say: "More. More."

His words were like music. Sounds that we had dared not consider, believing perhaps that he might never talk again. The first verbal statements from him in over a week. Incredible. Impossible. Raun had moved through it. This day he had re-created the world again . . . choosing more positively and will-fully than ever before. He was with us. Allowing himself to be tickled and laughing. Jumping while holding my hands. Using language. And when I touched my nose, he said: "Nose."

When Suzi touched her hair and asked him what it was, he answered: "Hair."

And as one of the dogs came charging through the door into the room, he announced: "Sacha."

He had never used these words before on his own. Yes, he had heard them often. And yes, he had repeated them on cue . . . but he had never been the originator, the first speaker. In the kitchen, Raun asked for water by distinctly saying: "Water."

And then after he drank the contents in the glass, he said: "More."

We were stunned. We could not move fast enough each time he uttered his request. He casually pointed to the end of Suzi's cigarette and spoke another new word emphatically: "Hot."

It was as if he could not contain himself from naming and saying everything he knew. He did not confine himself to the five words that he had learned to use over the last month. He was now responding verbally to all the images and words that we had carefully and repetitiously presented to him over the past fourteen weeks. At the end of the week, Suzi and I sat down to record every word that he had spoken. The list was spectacular. Raun's active vocabulary expanded in this one week from a mere seven words to an incredible seventy-five.

132

Later during that first morning, Raun took Suzi's hand and said: "Come."

And where did Raun take his mother? Into the den, to begin a session, to communicate his wanting. He walked over to the closet and clearly asked for a puzzle. She responded immediately. When she took out only one, he indicated that he wanted more of them . . . all of them. She unloaded the closet onto the floor. He sat down directly in front of her and waited to begin. Before Suzi had a chance to separate the puzzles, he grabbed the form of the cow and quickly moaned in a fashion familiar to him. "Mooooo. Mooooo."

Raun was telling us loud and clear. He wanted to work again . . . to learn, to interact, to talk. In many ways, his desire and enthusiasm were stronger. A new forcefulness came from him. A new lucidity about his wants and relating to people.

133

Ten

LOG: TWENTIETH WEEK—SCHEDULE RESUMED IN FULL

Note:

This week has been like a roller-coaster ride . . . first, Raun is super-cooperative and in contact, then he is detached and unpredictable. Shows irritation and annoyance often. Much fluctuation in moods and behavior patterns.

Observations:

—Makes more of an attempt to use language

—Seems to really enjoy working sessions and actively solicits coming into his work room so that his sessions can begin

—Has begun to bring strangers into his work room to show them his puzzles and games . . . he will often do them with new people

—Effective language (operative use on his own to his own tempo to express wants. Words said with varying degrees of clarity. Some he uses to express wants and others in naming appropriate objects when he is asked to identify things). Active vocabulary: hair, nose, ears, eyes, teeth,

134

neck, arm, hand, finger, shoe, leg, head, penis, come, yes, out, no, more, flower, water, bottle, light, hot, up, down, chair, don't do that, pillow, music, rug, ball, crow, doggie, duck, piggie, lamb, goat, cow, hen, horse, boy, penguin, deer, cat, bunnie, donkey, carriage, closet, baby, dolly, drum, book, barrel, fish, clock, Daddy, Mommy, Thea, Bryn, Maire, Sacha, Nancy, clap hands, piano, door, belly, pretty, juice, Bonnie, stop, banana, go, upstairs

—Receptive vocabulary is much larger . . . can also follow complex commands, i.e., "Raun, please get me the ball, pick it up and give it to Mommy."
—Initiates more playing with members of the family
—More interest in going outside and taking walks
—Has become fascinated with license plates on cars and letters in general
—Has started eating this week with a spoon by himself
—Will take puzzles and play with them by himself with obvious enjoyment
—Still hypnotically fascinated with music
—Climbs on the chair for a piggy-back ride
—Plays ring-around-the-rosie

Additional Notes:
—Dribbling very much and keeps his tongue out of his mouth. But he does respond when asked to put it back into his mouth.

* * *

What happened? What did it mean? To withdraw and then return. To try the old and, perhaps, to compare it with the new feelings and experiences. No matter how difficult and confusing the last six months had been, they had had their own special brand of excitement and enrichment. Raun had come to discover and participate actively in our lives. He knew now that he could sort and digest his perceptions . . . that he could be a participant and move out beyond his walls.

135

* * *

LOG: TWENTY-SECOND WEEK—SAME SCHEDULE

Note:

Raun is still working well, although inconsistently. At twenty-two months, he exhibits a new mischievousness and is constantly testing authority. With us, with his peer group and siblings, testing his will. We note a great willingness to interact socially, but he still wants to be in control. Teachers showing him how effective, exciting and useful his participating is for him. Imitation exercises back in full force. When we follow his clapping hands or banging the table or shaking our heads, he becomes animated and joyful. When we try to initiate the same, he will only follow upon specific request.

Observations:

—Increased propensity toward doing the same things . . . likes to do same activities over and over again

—Since he showed interest in letters (license plates), we have introduced letters into his exercises (block letters and magnetic letters on board); we have started to teach him the four letters of his name

—Now when you ask him who wants the water or juice, he will say "me" and will indicate further by banging his hands on his chest

—Can now distinguish between hard and soft . . . can demonstrate comparisons

—Actively initiates his sessions

—Greater facility in learning new words . . . absorbs and retains faster

—Starting to teach him to take off his own clothes

—More involved interaction with our dogs; plays more actively

—Aggressive game playing with Bryn and Thea; excellent peer playing with Thea.

136

*   *   *

In this, his twenty-second month, as we had previously arranged (in our effort to touch every base), we took Raun back to one of the hospitals for an electroencephalogram. We were ushered into a special wing and met with five staff members, each of whom had different job responsibilities. Two were actually charged with administering the test. I explained to them that before I could allow this testing to proceed I wanted to be shown exactly where and how the examination was performed. I was concerned with anything that might be frightening or antiproductive to Raun.

The technician took me into a computer read-out room. One wall was a two-way mirror which would allow us to observe Raun and the testing procedure. They would try to do the test with him fully awake. If, owing to his age, he moved around too much, they would sedate him mildly. Once he was resting comfortably on the bed, twenty-two electrodes would be taped to various parts of his head: one on each of his temples, one in the center of his forehead and the remainder spread out over his head. Seven charts would be taken, with one additional reading to compensate for any movements which would distort the readings. These electrodes track brain waves through electrical impulses. If there were breaks or irregularities in patterns, then certain types of brain damage would be detected.

In this antiseptic environment, Raun was unusually hyperactive. The nurses played with him in and out of the testing area. We left and our son remained there, perfectly at home. They administered tiny doses of sedative orally for three hours until he finally fell asleep. Then, after all the electrodes were pasted on his head and the machinery was put into action, Raun awoke for only ten seconds—long enough to look around and pull all the wires from his head. They began again as soon as he settled back into a quiet sleep.

The harmless sedative left Raun dizzy and disoriented for over two days. And the results of the tests were as expected for a child like Raun . . . the readings were normal for a child his age and unrevealing.

*　　*　　*

LOG: TWENTY-FOURTH WEEK—SAME SCHEDULE

Observations:

—He will now follow us in the games that we initiate
—Exposed him to four new puzzles (each with thirteen pieces)—he did them quickly and with great ease
—Drooling less and less
—Starting to put words together, i.e., "thank you," and "I wanna"
—Acquired more words and participating more verbally
—In park, more inquisitive with other children . . . note his interest in more-passive children, will approach with great zest, touching them and hugging them or gently pinching their cheeks
—Learned to identify colors—red, white, blue, green, yellow, black, orange and purple . . . could demonstrate how he could generalize this and associate different objects of the same color
—Stacks blocks very well now—six high
—Turns a six-sided insertion toy box to find the right hole for a form (the box has a total of thirty different shape forms)
—Waves and says hello as well as goodbye
—Moved chair across an entire room so that he could climb on it in order to reach a cup on the counter.

*　　*　　*

The next week, Nancy made her dramatic and unexpected announcement: she had decided to leave the program; to go on to other projects. The mood was heavy with her hesitancy and tension. Her eyes were jumping along the floor and finally fixed on the ceiling. Plagued by her own choice? Perhaps she believed that she "should" continue or that she would be unhappy

138

if she did not. Her words of goodbye were spoken as if she had rehearsed them, repeating her pronouncements over and over again in her head until she had molded them for proper impact. She wanted to remain our friend, but sever the teaching aspect. She feared that her departure as Raun's teacher would result in her losing relationships she had treasured for over five years.

Her dark, long hair hid part of her face as she folded her arms across her chest. She was resolved in her decision, but her voice was thin and her body slumped down in the chair. It was okay, we told her. Our love and our relationship were not contingent on her continuing in the program. She would always be part of this family, part of Raun and his thrust. The connection would be there as long as she wanted it. By evening's end, all of us had digested the announcement and its ramifications.

Our immediate concern was for Raun. What would this mean for him? Although we valued Nancy's contribution and involvement, we promptly concentrated on filling the gap instead of lingering on the loss. She had been with us for many months and this juncture marked an inevitable reshuffling of our teaching group.

Within several days, after numerous interviews, we began to train another teacher-facilitator, who was introduced slowly as we phased out Nancy.

Raun's reaction was instantaneous. He was sensitive and intuitively alert, rejecting Louise, his new teacher, and participating with her inconsistently. Hours and hours of being with her were needed before he would begin to work with her. He made a modest protest, which, perchance, escalated when he caught a cold. His use of language diminished, becoming inconsistent and sporadic. He reintroduced rocking, but only mildly. We encouraged Louise and ourselves. If there's a loss that he is feeling, help him through it. Be open. Be sensitive to him. Catch every message.

During this period of readjustment, Raun developed a fetish for the garbage pails in the kitchen and bathroom. For two days, he continually asked for them. On the third day, we went to a store and purchased every pail in sight. Large ones and small ones. Pails of different shapes and colors. Fifteen rubber containers. His reaction of delight was immediate and overwhelming. He laughed and yelled when we presented them to him.

He jumped up and down and actually clapped. Pails everywhere. Stacked in tall towers against the wall. Inserted neatly
into each other on the floor. He adopted a yellow pail as his hat.
The large red one became a hideout. The small blue one was
always being filled with water. He was diverted and involved.
Nancy continued to visit on random occasions. Raun, who was
always glad to see her, had come to fully accept her absence as
teacher-therapist.

More solid than ever before, Raun continued to build his own
strength and power, assuming a new posture of independence.
I felt the time had come for a leave of absence . . . after pressing
Suzi for weeks, she finally agreed to take an extended weekend
off from our intense schedule. We felt that Raun was fully capable of holding his own . . . of absorbing change and growing with
it.

Once that decision had been made, dramatic preparations
got underway. Elaborate schedules were arranged for both
Bryn and Thea to have friends and activities. My brother and
his wife offered to take the girls for a day. Beautiful. Then Suzi
constructed Raun's schedule exactly as it had been with the
only change being to replace her. Maire would live at our house
while working with Raun as usual. Louise would simply continue. Nancy agreed to return to help. And then Victoria. Big
Vic, who, for months now had become close to us and the
program, also wanted to participate and try again. Although she
and Raun had had difficulty during the summer, she believed
that she had since learned a great deal more from us and that
she could be much more effective now. After long and intense
talks, we decided that she could replace Suzi in the morning
sessions. We had arranged for a total force of six people to cover
and comfort these three children. Secure, but with a sense of
daring, we departed.

The next morning, Vikki arrived to find Raun more verbal
and communicative than ever before. All was gentle and flowing. He was affectionate and working well in his session. The
hours whizzed by as the two of them glided through the games
and the toys. Nancy and Maire handled the afternoon and evening shifts. Then, slowly, there was a change during that first
day. On several occasions he called for us. Even though only
half a day had elapsed, it represented the longest single period

of time during which he had not seen and not interacted with his mother since the inception of our program. He sensed the difference. His glow dimmed; his early excitement turned into dullness. Throughout this relatively mild withdrawal, they noticed his tendency to cling to them. The special way he held their hands very tightly, squeezing their legs as he hugged them. Grabbing at physical contact with a new force. And yet, in this effort, he seemed to be losing his own equilibrium.

"Can I help, Raun? Do you want something?"

They all solicited him. The reaction . . . nonexistent. He slid further into the well of his own thoughts and feelings. Even Bryn and Thea noted the change and tried to intercede. Bryn suggested that Maire call us because she believed that Raun was sad that we were gone. Their concern mounted and so did the melancholy mood.

Vikki returned the following morning and brought Raun downstairs. Again he was alert. Enthusiastic. A noticeable improvement over his twilight heaviness. This time, before reaching the den, he became mesmerized by the photographs of Suzi and me hanging on the wall. Carefully he approached them as if he were a hunter stalking his prey. Deliberate. Then, in a great burst of excitement and joy, he pointed to my picture and yelled: "Daddy! Daddy!"

As he continued to repeat my name, his voice trailed off into a whisper as his face became darkened and strained. Over and over he called to me through the photograph. Each utterance bounced off the glass unanswered. I was lost to him and he knew it. He was confused, perhaps even fearful. Quickly, he pivoted his body and faced Suzi's portrait. With the same incredible enthusiasm he shouted: "Mommy! Mommy! Mommy!"

Then, as before, the words started to fall limply from his lips until they too were almost inaudible. He went on repeating his chant, not wanting to give up. Daring to come closer to Suzi's photo . . . touching her nose with his small hands, moving his fingers up and down her face and then caressing her hair in its one-dimensional world. Trying to make sense out of it . . . trying to make love. He pulled his fingers back and stared at them . . . feeling cheated by the illusion. Then his eyes concentrated on Suzi's as if he were trying to bring her back. A willed reincarnation. Finally, his hands dropped heavily to his sides and he

141

became lost in his own gaze. Several minutes passed in silence, then he suddenly turned to Vikki and said: "Puzzle, Bikki. Come. Wanna puzzle."

Vikki smiled warmly at the little man as she took his hands into hers. Stroking them. Together.

More than just searching for his parents . . . Raun was searching for himself.

The session began in the den. Although he did cooperate, he was lifeless and distracted. When he heard a sound from another part of the house, he would stop precisely on that cue and listen intently. Then, aloud but essentially to himself, he uttered: "Mommy? Mommy?"

Vikki began to speak to him as he stared at the doorway: "Mommy gone away, but Mommy coming back. A few days, that's all. Mommy and Daddy will be back soon."

Raun glanced at her with the same question: "Mommy?"

A query or a statement? Perhaps a prayer. Haunting him. Riveting his attention to the people who were missing. Focused and exploring. Raun then closed his mouth as Suzi had taught him and began to hum. And he rocked from side to side, soothing himself and preparing. Like a recording on playback, Raun began to sing his entire repertoire of songs that Suzi had taught him. He sang one song after another without interruption. "Three Blind Mice." "Over There, Over There." " 'A'-You're Adorable." "Splish Splash." "Tie a Yellow Ribbon." And all the others. Notations of love. Familiar. The warm associations were a source of comfort.

Vikki sang along with him. Yet, with each passing hour, she knew he was slipping . . . but in a different way than in the past. He was definitely not resorting to his elaborate system of autistic behaviors. Both Nancy and Maire were becoming even more upset by the continuing strain on Raun. Vikki was extremely disturbed, but pushed to stay in touch.

By evening, he was seemingly more depressed, but nevertheless continued to participate though without real fire and energy.

By morning, Raun was even more polarized. Not like any of the previous reversals. Not specifically withdrawn or out of touch; he appeared angry. After breakfast, Vikki and Raun began the session. For several minutes, he cooperated and then suddenly stopped short. He was closing a door in himself and opening another. He peered directly into Victoria's eyes . . . a blast of defiance. He was thinking rapidly and with great purpose.

Another jump; Raun was changing.

Grabbing the edge of the puzzle, he threw it and watched it break apart as it hit the wall and the pieces flew in every direction. Fireworks for the amusement of one little man. He knocked the blocks down and started throwing them in the air. Vikki smiled at him and put her hand out to him. No response. He pulled the leg from under one of the chairs and toppled the piece of furniture. He ran to the desk and pushed off all the papers and books.

"What do you want, Raun? Tell Vikki. Vikki help you."

He answered her with more pushing and throwing. More drooling and short, fleeting periods of staring. There was more overturning of furniture as he charged each piece like a bull fighting for its life. As he pushed things over, he screamed out their names.

"Chair!"

"Book!"

"Blocks!"

"Table!"

Vikki's mind was racing as if she were on speed. What to do? Do it now. Now. Pushing herself, processing and reprocessing, fumbling through the quicksand of data, looking for something to grab on to . . . the way out. Thinking back to the hundreds of conversations with Suzi and me. The descriptions of how we made contact through intense involvement . . . doing it without disapproval or expectations. Remembering the early phases of our program during the summer. Intervention. Love. Reserve the judgments.

Allow him to be.

Flashes of watching Suzi during the endless hours of trying to make contact without any visible effect. Suzi's words bouncing back across the threshold of time. "He knows when you're sincere or insincere," she always maintained. "It's part of our attitudes which we give off like an odor . . . which we communicate with the tone of our voice, the texture of our body language, our gestures, eye movements and facial expressions.

143

When I imitate Raun, I'm not putting him on . . . I'm really involved. I'm caring. I want him to know that I love him, that he's okay and I really believe it. So, when I rock, I become as much a part of it as he is. I'm there for him and for me . . . and he knows that."

The notes sounded and reverberated throughout the membranes of her mind. An overture. Vikki jumped to her feet and turned all the furniture right side up and then immediately proceeded to knock everything over. Raun watched amazed for several seconds. Tactics being formulated. Then he joined in. As she moved faster than he did, one time he came directly up to her, pushed her out of the way and said: "Go away. Go away!"

She did not resist him, but moved away from him to another chair and threw it over. As she became more and more involved, lost in the growing fury of her own energy, she went outside the room and started throwing pieces over throughout the entire house. Raun ran parallel to her, flipping everything out of his way. The mad rampage of two gifted people working out a bizarre pantomime of love and anger. Raun's intensity became greater as his breathing became heavier and beads of sweat decorated his face. More than a temper tantrum . . . a statement.

In isolated moments, he would stop all the frenetic activity to walk over to Vikki and hug her leg. Then, pushing off again and continuing. After two hours of going back and forth, Raun finally drifted over through the exhaustion and put his head on her lap. She was still panting as she kissed him and stroked his head. Then she asked him if he wanted to go back into the den to work. He straightened up, took her hand and stated with great authority: "Come."

Raun sat down opposite her in the room. He kept rubbing his eyes as he worked the puzzles and turned the pages of his books. From time to time, he would smile at her as she talked to him. Then, after about half an hour, he stood up and walked over to her. He leaned his head on her shoulder for several minutes. Lingering.

That evening, when Nancy tried to put him to sleep, he cried frantically. She brought him back downstairs . . . letting him move about and waiting for him to tire. It was obvious he was stoking the fire. Keeping himself awake. Perhaps he was concerned that she too might disappear as did his parents. Exhaustion began to overtake him. His legs seemed uncertain and carried his body with a drunken imbalance. Giving in, he put his head on Nancy's lap and fell asleep standing. A contemporary Renoir, colors earthy and muted, the hard edges softly rounded by the mellowness of a little boy trying to make it the best he could. Stay with me. Love me. Help me be here. The messages were emphatic.

When Suzi and I returned late the next day Raun was already asleep. We found Nancy and Maire drawn and drained. They talked as if they had been through the mill . . . worn and wasted. Both were concerned and caring for Raun, yet somehow they were ignoring what appeared, to us, as a dramatic and beautiful event. We began to laugh in our own excitement as they described it. Maire, slightly outraged, threatened to leave if we did not stop smiling. A long and intense three-hour rap followed. Later, after I explained what I saw, we were all enjoying the fruits of this special weekend.

It had been a learning experience for all of us . . . and most importantly for Raun. Unlike all the notations in the literature or even the experiences in our own immediate past, Raun had done the unexpected. He had chosen people instead of the autistic symptoms. He had picked contact instead of self-stimulating isolation. He had showed anger instead of giving up for what might have been easier. He had dared to hold fast to his wanting and had expressed it over and over again. This weekend Raun had made, on his own, a daring movement. Even under pressure and confusion, he had opted for his people and the world of contact.

In the morning, Raun was elated to see us. Both of us went into his room to take him out of his crib.

"Mommy. Mommy. Daddy."

Smiling. Saying our names again and again. Showing us his stuffed doggie and his animal book, which he kept in his bed. Excited and enormously happy.

Raun looked at Suzi and said: "Hugga. Hugga."

She threw her arms around his tiny body and caressed him. His hands gently pressed around her neck. They lingered to-

145

gether, enjoying, loving. After several minutes, Suzi untied herself from him. Still beaming, he turned toward me and said: "Hugga. Hugga, Daddy."

I picked him up in my arms and pressed him to me . . . with his head on my shoulder. He tightened his grip around my shoulders. Loving this little boy brought the best in me alive.

Then he received a piggy-back ride downstairs. He motioned for Suzi to take him into the den, even before his breakfast. He wanted to play his games . . . with all their familiarity, intensity and richness.

Vikki was formally reintroduced into the program the following week to become a participating teacher-facilitator. In addition, we began to develop two other enthusiastic young people . . . orienting them to our concepts, exploring their attitudes, helping them investigate their beliefs and teaching them our approach. We moved very smoothly.

We were all energized. Involved. We put the classes back into the full schedule. Raun was working puzzles with great rapidity. He was identifying objects and colors quickly and emphatically. He had developed an interest in dolls, and in fact, had now begun actively to play with a small Raggedy Ann. On many occasions, Raun would cheer himself after completing an exercise, yelling and clapping his hands for his accomplishments. His solicitation for physical interaction and contact increased daily. More piggy-back rides, jumping up and down, more tickling and rolling together on the bed. His language ability, acquisition of new words and the use of small phrases and sentences increased.

Upon specific recommendation of a friend, we decided to make another try to go outside of ourselves. Although all that we had developed and accomplished was the result of our own inventiveness, creativity and energy, we wanted always to remain open. Perhaps there would be others who could show us new directions. We would go to anyone, anywhere, who we believed could help us, help our son. But to this day we've walked on uncharted ground.

We visited another "special" school. It was created and designed specifically for children with learning, emotional and behavioral problems. Well staffed with involved personnel, it was characterized by an attitude of efficiency. Raun's reaction, when placed in a class, was poor. Indeed, so were Suzi's and mine. Children were pushed and pulled into different activities. They were physically manipulated and directed. One child who wanted to leave an exercise was actually held by force in his chair. Many of them seemed completely lost in the frenzied and hectic atmosphere. Perhaps, under the circumstances, this was the best they could do. Yet chances of recovering a lost life here seemed slim, if not impossible.

Once again, we would be moving on by ourselves. No other loving and learning program existed that was more intense and individually appropriate than the one we had designed. We had nothing to prove, but so much to gain from our wanting and allowing. There was yet no other place or environment based on the Attitude: "To love is to be happy with."

Epilogue

It was the thirtieth week of our intervention program. Raun was twenty-four months old. He was still moving ahead at a rapid pace. Still being enriched on a seventy-five-hour-per-week schedule. We all were watching and listening as he used language and communicated in a useful and meaningful context. Through the barrier of his own encapsulation. He had found the new pathways, opened new channels and now addressed the world. In a total of only seven short months, there has been a lifetime of movement.

Two years old. We decided on another work-up, to be performed at the same institution that had seen him four months before, when he was twenty months old. We went back into the same room with the same people.

In the lobby, Raun was lively, articulate and moving. As we waited for our appointment, one of the staff members on the work-up team saw us and came over to say her hellos. As she looked at Raun, she seemed startled. Her eyes gaped out of their sockets as her mouth dropped. Raun was moving from the couch to the chair to the lamp. As he moved, he was naming each item that he touched.

"I can't believe it," the woman exclaimed. "I can't believe

148

this is the same child we saw four months ago. I'd never have believed it was possible. Oh, this is just wonderful."

She led us back down long corridors. The sharp turns and the monotonous sameness of the walls . . . monuments. Windows broke the severity with sunshine and trees. Raun ran ahead of us, almost as if he were anticipating this meeting and the examination, as if wanting to get there. We entered the room greeting the same staff members we had seen before. Raun looked at each one and said "Hi" to one of the doctors that addressed him. They looked back and forth at one another . . . their expectations and what they were observing were obviously at odds. They were excited and confused. Was this the same child?

Extremely active, but in complete control, Raun continued the remarkable display of his awareness and battery of knowledge . . . but without solicitation or reward. He walked over to the couch and said easily: "Couch. Couch. Yellow couch."

Then he stepped over to a chair and pointed at it, saying: "Chair. Blue."

Then he flitted over to another and another exclaiming: "Chair. Red chair. Blue. Yellow chair."

Suddenly, he stopped as if to survey the environment for reactions. He flashed from face to face, studying expressions. Then, he pointed to the ceiling and said: "Light."

Pointing authoritatively to the floor beneath his feet he uttered: "Floor."

And so he continued before the enlarged and absorbing eyes of this special hospital staff. Even I was stunned by his energy and purposefulness. Although it seemed impossible, it was as if he knew exactly why he was there.

One of the doctors, who had previously shown no particular affection toward Raun during the last series of tests, held him on his lap and said with great warmth: "Hello, Raun . . . you're a very good boy."

Then he put him down as if to avoid becoming prejudiced in his assessment and evaluation. He suggested we begin.

They took Raun through a three-hour series of examinations and interviews. Another Gesell charting of the exercises and performances. In the end, the head diagnostician and his associates faced us in their intake room. They began by explaining to us that they had fully expected us to return at this juncture with

149

a child who would, at best, be functioning at half his age level and who would be mentally retarded and withdrawn. Only four months ago, when they had seen Raun at twenty months of age, he was functioning limitedly on a level appropriate for an eight-month-old in language and socialization.

Now the tests and scoring showed a child who, at twenty-four months, was functioning in every way at his appropriate age level. Even better! In over half the tests, Raun functioned at the thirty-to thirty-six-month age level. These four months had marked an incredible and real developmental surge of sixteen to twenty-six months. The dull, encapsulated and unreachable little boy was now articulate and obviously very intelligent.

The doctors were dramatically impressed and surprised. Raun's accomplishments had pushed at the walls of their professional experience. They would have said it was improbable, if not impossible.

The senior staff doctor weighed the results together with our attitude, our articulated beliefs, the concept of endless possibilities. He and his staff members suggested that we develop a program with them to try to help other children. Beautiful; we would consider it. Perhaps, in the near future, it could become a reality.

Our meeting ended with an ironic twist. The head diagnostician resurrected a fractured piece of advice. He thought we could ease off or discontinue our program . . . but now the reason was he judged Raun to be well-adjusted and, in fact, exceptionally bright. Incredible! Had they not understood?

Raun, in many ways, was still working twice as hard as another child would while performing the same tasks. He was still repairing himself, experimenting with his perception and developing his thinking apparatus. Still volatile and vulnerable. We knew that a severe cold, an injury, some new pressure, an unpredictable and uncontrollable sensory bombardment could trigger his retreat . . . that any one of those retreats could be forever. But the only thing that really mattered was the beauty and the wonderment of this very moment. Now.

The story of Raun unfolding. Just beginning as his flowering abounds. The smile of Raun. The voice of Raun. The sensitivity of Raun. His behavior is still marked by his specialness. The autistic symptoms have faded, but have not entirely disappeared. He had preserved those parts of himself that he wanted

150

to take with him. This had, in fact, been his journey toward our world.

*   *   *

Sitting. Waiting. In that hospital lobby with Raun before that last examination. Suzi on the couch watching Raun. I, in my world, climbing the brick walls with my eyes, still searching for answers. As we sat there, a little girl and her mother came walking past. The little girl broke away from her mother's grasp and ran directly to Suzi, who opened her arms. Eyes were teal blue and razor sharp. Suzi stroked her face gently and began talking to her quietly. The child just gazed into Suzi's eyes and touched her head to Suzi's. They were like two old friends saying hello on the stone floor. The mother then came over and without saying a word took the child's hand and directed her toward the door. All this time, the little girl kept looking back at Suzi.

Later, we inquired about this child. We were told that she was autistic, a patient with whom they were having no success because of her marked lack of interest in people. Peculiar. Myopic. Perhaps, this little girl knew. Perhaps, when an attitude is so much a part of someone, verbal communication is totally unnecessary.

Little girl blue. Raun Kahlil. There is no real place. They're so young and so adrift. They are dealt with en masse, statistically. They are pushed and pulled instead of followed. The heartache. The lifetime incarceration. The fortune of money expended for custodial care. The wasted energy. Raun, perhaps, is beyond all that now; for him there are continually evolving horizons. Others can share in it if they are recognized early before their sensibilities and disabilities create an emotional shell that could become almost impregnable.

Autism could be a learning tree, an incredible hybrid that is distinctly humane. These special little people can be reached. Their self-contained systems can be merged with the delights of our world. Perhaps, for us too, this is a new beginning. Raun Kahlil has become a mover and teacher of us all.

In each of us, there is that specialness that is a gift to others.

THE BEGINNING

151

Epilogue II

.One year has elapsed, floating into the recent past as we continue our program on the basis of forty hours each week. The day to day sessions are more focused on exercising and stimulating an alert and active mind, rather than any specific attempt to upgrade our son's intellectual abilities. His thirst to learn is acute. He even greets the unstructured periods of his day with a vigorous capacity to relate to people and his environment.

Raun Kahlil is three years old and continues to soar. He is loving, happy, creative. And communicative. Each day he gives birth to a new sunrise. Raun loves life and life loves him back.

His enjoyment of people remains intense; he can speak in compound sentences of up to sixteen words. Six months ago, when he was two-and-a-half, we began to teach him to read. At this time, he can move through the book of a first grader, which is the equivalent to the skills of a child twice his age . . . a six year old. He can spell over three hundred words. Numbers and counting have worked their way into his world. Favored games include adding and subtracting using his fingers and his toes.

He creates fantasy characters from his imagination and can

role-play members of our teaching crew by imitating their voices and personality traits. As the magic of music weaves throughout his daily life, Raun explores the piano by duplicating songs he has been taught. He has also made this instrument his own by composing little songs . . . melodies and words.

Raun's energy is matched only by his happiness. His curiosity and his joy, his wisdom and his tranquility have touched us all . . . moved us all to places we've always wanted to be. For each of us, Raun has been a doorway into the quick of who we are and what we can be for each other.

Several months ago **Maire** announced her departure from our program in order to begin college. Her tears became the symbols of her caring. Watching Raun construct a small city out of blocks, she addressed us as if she were talking to herself: "I can't get used to the thought of leaving him . . . he's taught me so very much . . . you've taught me so much. You've all become such an important part of my life. I feel so changed, so loved. But somehow, I guess I know it's okay to leave. Raun's really doing it for himself now. He's on his own."

ACKNOWLEDGMENTS

I am deeply grateful to the man who first taught me the Option Method, and who, by his own request, wishes to remain anonymous.

There are no words to express my appreciation to Suzi, my wife, who not only lived this story but worked with me daily as my alter ego in the preparation of this book.

A sincere thanks is conveyed to Marvin Beck and Ellen Kanner, two very special people whose input enriched my manuscript. I also wish to thank Kitty Benedict, my editor, whose suggestions were invaluable, and Harper & Row, my publisher, who believed in this book from the very beginning.